Until Death Do

Us

Part!

A Mystery Novel

by

Gregory J.T. Simpson

Until Death Do Us Part!

Until Death Do Us Part! is
Published and Distributed by Creative Dreamers

For information, contact:
Creative Dreamers
4828 Redan Road
Suite 257
Stone Mountain, Georgia 30088
www.gjtsimpsonworld.com
Or e-mail us at creativedreamers@gjtsimpsonworld.com

ISBN: 0-971-0049-0-0

Printed in the United States of America

2nd Edition

Cover Model: Robert A. Price

To Janet,
Enjoy the RIDE!

My heart will always be divided into four equal and loving parts — Janet, Cree, Logan, and Chase are those special parts.

Until Death Do Us Part!

A wedding isn't supposed to mean as much to the groom as it does to the bride. I was taught that this was her day, her moment, and her time to be emotional. The second most important day in her life next to giving birth. As I watch my love walk down the chapel aisle toward me, no one could prove to me that this day was not my day also. Tall, beautiful, classy, and powerful, my lady is all that and more. To see the most magnificent woman God has blessed me with promise her love to me for better or worse, richer or poorer, in sickness and in health brought a tear to my eyes. I never thought that I could be so in love, and I've never been happier.

Prologue

"Good evening, beautiful! Are you missing me as much as I'm missing you?"

"Silly question, Noah. I can't wait until you get your fine black butt back to Atlanta and your primary job of taking care of me and this bratty little girl you've left me with."

"Tomorrow morning, Andrea. I'm catching the first flight out, and as far as our spoiled daughter is concerned, you're as much to blame as I am."

"Not true, handsome. I only pick her up when she's crying; you walk around with her cradled in your arms, just because you think she's beautiful. There will be no spoiling Ms. Thing tonight. I'm exhausted. I'm going to keep her up as close to my bedtime as possible and then give her a good bath right before I put her butt down. If this works out, I should be able to get a solid four or five hours of sleep before she wakes up for her next feeding. For some strange reason that not even you can explain, Ashley seems to not want to sleep through the night like she usually does when you're not home."

I laugh to myself and ignore her comment because I know Andrea's trying to do the guilt trip thing. "Sounds like a doable plan, Andrea, and I promise you that all of the sacrifices we've both made will pay off real soon. I think this trip will turn out to be a huge turning point in the life cycle of our business. But we'll get into that when I get home. Where is my daughter right now?"

"On the floor next to me sleeping peacefully. She's resting up now, so that she can spend half the night keeping me awake with her screaming demands for attention. Ashley is growing up much too fast for me and she's only nine months old this week. Are you sure you want to have another bundle of joy? One seems to be enough for my poor old soul."

"You're the incubator. You tell me when you're ready for another bundle of joy. I just know that I want a little boy, and the sooner, the better but I'm not going to demand that you produce right away."

"Did I hear you say demand?" Andrea asked, letting me hear the laughter in her voice.

"I missed loving you this past week," I continued ignoring her question and changing the subject entirely. "Am I allowed to sample the goodies when I get home?"

"Hell no, smart ass," Andrea answered playfully. "You just called me an incubator, and you think I'm going to let you enjoy the richness of my soul? How much money do you have? I may let you buy a little."

"You're my wife, why do I have to pay to play? Me begging for the good stuff should be price enough," I said, enjoying our game. "You should be paying me, 'cause you know I got skills."

"Noah, anything you do know about loving a woman, I taught you. And I still haven't been paid in full for those lessons, but I'll give you a discount when you get home if you say the magic words."

"I love you, Andrea."

"Bingo. The sweet stuff is yours, baby. Hurry home, because my tired ass is missing you."

Chapter 1

I got there early in the morning on a moonless night. I like working this time of the morning. Article I read years ago talked about the deep-sleep period for most folks being between 2:00 and 4:00 A.M. For the jobs I get paid for, this seemed like the most humane time.

I been described by folks on the street as a nameless, heartless spirit. I just think I'm a badass nigga trapped in a small-ass midget body. I'm rolling with my ass-kicking all black working shit on, rubber-sole shoes, loose-fitting cotton pants, knit hat with the eyes and mouth cut out, custom-made leather jacket with hidden pockets for my tools, turtleneck sweater, and black gloves. The only thing that don't match my purple-black skin is my silver-gray eyes and hair that I guess I got from some dumb-ass slave master, generations ago.

The house I'm looking for is in one of them uppity black sections of Atlanta. They say this Hidden Hills hood covers over one hundred acres and got more than fifteen different subdivisions and a thousand plus homes. You'd never catch a nigga like me living here. When are niggas going to learn? They always going to be niggas no matter where they live.

The thing pissing me off the most right now is the fact that my so-called boss didn't give me no damn time to case this kill. But money talks and bullshit walks, and he's going to pay a good bit for this one. I don't know much about his ass, even though I work for him. The word at the club is that he's untouchable. Now, this don't mean shit to me since I'm in the profession of touching the untouchables. The only thing I give a damn about anyway is the Benjamins, and they always come as promised. One of the few things I don' learned from the white boy is how to hide my money. As soon as I get my bennies, I place them in my offshore account. Ain't no fucker can touch my money once I make that deposit.

Mr. Mysterious did tell me this kill would be a no-brainer. I fucked up by waiting so close to the killing time to find the house, but I'm here now, and she got no idea how close she is to meeting the devil himself.

Her crib is surrounded on the backside by the golf course that snakes throughout the entire subdivision. Why a bunch of niggas would want to live on a damn golf course is beyond me. They should know by now white folks don't want them playing they sports.

The house is a two-story gray stucco with huge windows that run across the entire back of the second floor, which faces the golf course. I circled the block looking for a in and out as well as a place to hide my ride. It ain't really my ride but the dude I borrowed it from won't know it's missing until he wakes up in the morning.

Being a typical home owner in Atlanta, she had the alarm company signs posted all over the front and back of the house, but she didn't have any of the floodlights that are installed all over the house turned on.

After parking the ride on the other side of the golf course, I cross the backyard green and work my way back to the house. After checking out the cheap alarm company signs I figure that all of the lower-floor doors and windows got alarms but not the upstairs windows. Adding motion detectors and window alarms on the top floor were usually more than most Joes were willing to pay for.

Normal folk get so comfortable in their hundred-thousand-dollar homes, protected by their $24.95 a month security system. Talk about a false sense of security. I been breaking into these houses since grade school, even went so far as to work for one of them national home-security companies for a couple of months, just to get the upper hand for gigs like this one. Luck's on my side tonight 'cuz the suction cups I bought along for my hands and knees work better on stucco than any other surface. I pick the room in the darkest part of the house with a full-window entrance. I check one more time to make sure the glass-cutting tool is where I put it earlier and start up the wall.

It only takes about sixty seconds to climb the wall and position myself where I can see the entire room. I can't see much but I can make out that it's a baby's nursery, complete with a pink crib and all the extras. Fuck! That asshole didn't tell me the lady had a kid. I don't see a motion detector or window alarm connected to the window, and I can't tell if there's a baby in the crib from here. I don't see a light for one of them damn baby monitors, though. The last thing I need now is for Momma to hear me climbing through the window on one of them damn things.

I check the window, and it ain't locked, so I don't need my glasscutter. After quietly slipping into the room, I check out the crib. Damn, a baby, and as close as I could tell, a little girl about nine or ten months old. That asshole knows my rules, and the main one is I don't do kids for any reason or amount of money. Hell, I ain't worrying about this now. He didn't pay for the kid anyway, so Moms' the only one getting put to sleep permanently tonight.

I check the outer hall that leads straight through the den and past those big-ass windows and ended in what looks like the master bedroom. Lowering myself to the floor, I crawled through the den to the doorway of the bedroom, which was open.

This room is pitch-black but I can make out a king-size bed and the outline of a body. As my eyes continue to get used to the dark, I can see her face on the pillow at the head of the bed.

Damn, this bitch is beautiful. She's a dark-chocolate sister with long, brown hair and white folks' looks, pointed nose, high cheekbones, and thin lips. I always been attracted to the more chocolate variety, and this sister is definitely the chocolate color I like. If this shit wasn't given to me so screwed up, I would love to lay a little pipe of my own before I do her up permanently. But, the last thing I want is to get caught with my pants down screwing some bitch I'm supposed to be killing, 'specially since I ain't too thrilled about doing this last-minute shit to start with. If I'd had time to case the joint and built a file on her, a little stray stuff wouldn't hurt.

I think about it for another second before I rise from the floor like a demon ghost in one of them horror movies and walk to the head of the bed. I take the nine-millimeter with the silencer from my holster, point it at her peacefully sleeping forehead and squeeze the trigger. Her body jumps at the moment of impact and now she has a pretty little entrance wound but the back of her head is splattered all over the headboard and bed. I shoot her again in the heart just to make sure.

I holster the nine and grab a plastic bag and a pair of scissors from one of my pockets. I cut a long lock of hair from her shattered head and put it in the bag. I quickly retrace my steps into the nursery and check on the still-sleeping baby one more time. She's a pretty little kid. I guess she got her good looks from Moms since I ain't never seen Daddy, but Moms should have kept her nose out of other people's business.

After exiting the way I came, I am halfway across the green before I get one of my kooky ideas. Taking the cell phone out of my pocket, I dial 911.

"Atlanta 911, is this an emergency?" the female attendant asks.

"I guess you could call it that. I just shot a bitch in her head and heart. She has a little brat in the other room. I will leave the phone so you imbeciles can trace the signal. I would also advise you to send over a couple of your female goons with some baby milk. You don't want the brat to wake up for her feeding with no milk, do ya? 'Cuz I promise you Moms won't be feeding her brat again."

Chapter 2

"Stephanie, do you have the boarding passes?"

"Of course I do, Noah, isn't that why you pay me the big bucks?" Stephanie replied with her eyes twinkling in their easygoing, mischievous way.

"Don't start with me, woman. You know it's too early in the morning for your sarcastic remarks," I exclaimed, trying to keep the playful smile on my face from spreading as we rushed through New York's Kennedy airport bound for the red-eye to Atlanta.

I don't care how early I rise or how insistent Stephanie is in ringing my room, I'm almost always late. It can be a meeting with my staff or this flight to Atlanta; I simply have no real concept for time. It's not entirely my fault on this occasion though. I had to stop and pick up a gift for Ashley, and this beautiful stuffed pink elephant just seemed to cry out her name to me from the concourse gift store. There are so many moments I've missed in her life already, and she's only nine months old. I can't say I didn't realize the sacrifices that would have to be made before I started this business. I knew that for my software company to survive, we as a family would have to make some major sacrifices.

"Are you ready to start practicing your breathing, Noah?" Stephanie whispered as she settled into her first-class window seat after helping me stow our briefcases and notebook computers in the overhead storage area. "At least I can't complain about our travel arrangements," she continued. "We do stay in the nicest hotels, and always fly first-class. I just don't know if I'll ever get used to your fear of flying. How could such a big, strong man turn to mush as soon as he sees an airplane?"

Stephanie is a pretty woman, thirty-two years old. Single, pale skin, long blond hair, with the typical middle-class housewife demeanor on the outside. This physical appearance fooled me in the beginning. Stephanie has turned out to be a dedicated and driven employee. Hiring her was one of the first things I did after moving back to Atlanta and getting my MBA in information technology from MIT. I originally met Stephanie during a summer internship when we were both working as assistant librarians at Morehouse College. She's always been the first one to the office and the last to leave. When we get this contract to design and support the billing and security software package for Hospital Management and its thirty private hospitals, she's the first person I plan to reward with a big fat bonus check.

As I eased into my seat I couldn't shake the rumbling in the pit of my stomach. I hate this feeling that always rears its ugly head when it comes to flying. There are really only two things I hate about flying, the takeoff and the landing, which you would never guess by my cool expression, or at least that's what I hoped to be displaying. By the time we had taxied down the runway and were given permission to lift off, Stephanie was snoring softly. I, on the other hand, was practicing my breathing and focusing on helping the plane achieve its maximum altitude.

After a surprisingly smooth departure on my part as well as the plane's, I relaxed for a minute then allowed my body to breathe on its own without my explicit instructions. It didn't take long afterward for me to fall into my self-analyzing mode. I began by critiquing myself on the presentation I had given the day before. I've always found this personal assessment of my presentations the best way of improving myself for the next contract proposal. My team and I had worked hard over the last six months on the software and contract foundation in conjunction with the team from Hospital Management. The chance to design the operating software and provide support for state and private hospitals would allow my company, HSD, Inc., for the first time since its inception, to have a truly profitable future.

Presenting the software was a breeze. I've never had a problem speaking to large groups of people, especially a group of upper-class, white male executives. For some reason my presence seems to throw them for a loop and before they can re-adjust, I've usually stolen the show. I've spent a lot of time over the years wondering what exactly it is about me that unnerves so many of my white male clients. I've never been able to see myself as an imposing figure, but at six-foot-one and two hundred and twenty pounds, almost everybody else does.

I still spend a useless amount of time wondering if it's my size, heritage, or the fact that I'm a highly educated black man that creates this uneasiness for most white folks. If I had a dollar for every person who asked me if I played football, I could probably pay off my overhead for the next three months. Not that this assumption has not helped me. For some unearthly reason, white folks are more inclined to accept a black male as a part of their world if he's an athlete. They conveniently forget that if they saw this same man walking down the street, they would politely go out of their way to avoid him. And the reality is I'm probably the last person anyone who knew me years back would pick for any sort of sport.

I only weighed about one hundred and fifty pounds when I graduated from high school and was voted class nerd unanimously four years running. Being known as "Professor" in an all black inner-city school wasn't the most positive aspect of my teenage years. I always knew I was smarter than most of my classmates and quite a few of the teachers, too.

Once I went to college, I still had a hard time finding an equal. The only thing that kept me grounded was my pops. He had no problem reminding me that just because I had book sense didn't mean that life was mine for the taking. "Sleepy" as my father is affectionately called because of his droopy eyes never missed an opportunity to remind me of his number one rule. "Book sense is useless without common sense and street sense." My daddy is a proven veteran in the street-sense department, having grown up in one of the worst projects of New Orleans.

My father was also a hard man before he married my mother and moved to Atlanta. I'm still amazed by the fact that whenever we visit New Orleans, people still speak of my daddy with reverence. As an adult, I still like to hear of his adventures as a Black Panther in the turbulent sixties, but it has become so difficult to separate fiction from the truth. I do know for a fact that he was a major force in changing the way blacks are accepted today in white America. He didn't walk with Martin Luther King, Jr., or believe in the nonviolent approach.

I have been told many times how in a street fight my dad was the best. I guess this would be a lot more credible if Pops would authenticate some of the stories. But one of his unspoken rules is to never confirm or deny anything that would make him bigger or smaller than he really is. The only thing he would ever confirm was that if it weren't for the Black Panthers he would have never met my mother. I have no real memories of my mother, just images in my head from pictures I've seen of us together. God, I would give almost anything to remember her smell, the sound of her voice, or the smile on her face. She died in labor bringing my baby sister, Gina, into this world when I was about a year old.

Talking about my mother automatically sends my father into an immediate funk. I guess loving a woman fiercely is an inherited trait for the males in my family. The moment I met Andrea, I knew she was my eternal soul mate, and after five years of marriage I would still do anything for her and our beautiful daughter.

Everything about us has been against the given rules, even the way we met. Gina had been bugging me for two weeks straight to take her to Club Nexus, which had recently opened. Although I had just started my business and there were a million things to do, I agreed only to get her off my back. Club Nexus was a huge place, built in an abandoned warehouse in the heart of Atlanta. It had three different levels, and each floor offered a different type of music and clientele.

Gina knew I hated to dance but she still insisted that we do the dance club mix, which was on the very top floor. She always insisted on dancing with me first until she could scope out the attractive available men. I've been used many times over the years as a make-believe boyfriend to help her fend off the brothers she just didn't want to be bothered with.

While dancing with Gina, I noticed this beautiful, tall, dark skin sister with a tantalizing smile. I couldn't tell what kind of body she possessed because of the business suit she was wearing, but I did notice the lack of a wedding ring on her finger. She definitely made a brother use his imagination with the seductive way she moved. She continued to smile and look in my direction for the next three songs. Gina noticed this, too, and whispered to me, "That impolite bitch has no idea I'm just your sister and not your girlfriend. I don't like being disrespected, and if I were your girlfriend, she'd have a grade A ass whipping coming her way."

Gina disappeared after the third song, and I took my usual nightclub position at the bar, drinking Sprite. Minutes later, Andrea Houston walked off the dance floor and introduced herself. Ten minutes into the conversation, I told Andrea that she would be my wife. I've never felt so stupid for saying and doing the things we did that first night together, but I've never experienced anything more comfortable either. That night we broke every rule we were ever taught, from never opening oneself up to anyone, especially not a stranger in a nightclub, to never falling in love and going to bed the first night you meet someone. Andrea and I danced and talked till the early-morning hours. We had so much in common, from our professions to the fact that neither of us smoked, did drugs of any sort, or drank alcohol, to our last names. Andrea told me she never wanted to change her last name and when I told her my full name, Noah Houston, you couldn't have painted a bigger smile on her face.

I found out that Andrea was a systems engineer for a major computer firm in Atlanta. She understood my desire to own my own company, as well as visualize the concepts and direction in which I wanted to go before I could even finish describing them. After tracking Gina down and giving her the keys to my car, Andrea and I left in her car and headed for the nearest restaurant for coffee. As much as I wanted to take Andrea to the classiest place in Atlanta, there was only one spot open at four o'clock in the morning and that was the Waffle House.

Known for its ninety-nine-cent waffles and waitresses from hell, this would never be the place I'd take someone I wanted to impress, but Andrea didn't care. It was like she wanted to be with me as much as I wanted to be with her. I don't think there has ever been another night in my life before or after Andrea that I just didn't want the moment to end. It still feels like a dream when I look back at that night. We ended the morning at her house, in her bed. I had never met a woman as passionate and intense as Andrea, nor have I ever trusted a woman as totally as I did that night. Making love to her was like surrendering my entire soul, not caring if I'd ever get it back. Andrea and I were married three months later, and I have never considered being with another woman or a time when she would not be in my life. After the birth of our daughter, I really felt like I had been blessed under a special star.

"Excuse me, sir, would you mind waking up your companion and asking her to fasten her seat belt, we're about to land," the male flight attendant said, interrupting my introspection.

"Sure, no problem," I answered as I reached over and shook Stephanie out of her semi-deep sleep.

We landed in Atlanta fifteen minutes later and were halfway through its huge airport when my name was announced over the paging system, and I was told to report to the airport's security office.

"Stephanie why don't you go and get your luggage while I find out what major catastrophe has happened to mine."

"No problem. I'll also pick up the car if you give me the keys. You know I've been looking for a reason to drive that Jag of yours anyway," she replied with the same whimsical look that she saves just for me and my relationship with my car.

One of the things I bought after getting our house was my Jaguar. It was the first brand-new car I had ever purchased after a lifetime of clunkers that drove me crazy and left me abandoned on many a lonely highway road. While walking to a gas station after one such incident, I vowed that after I got this business going I would buy my dream car, which happened to be the Jaguar Vanden Plas. It's a long, stylish car with a deep blue leather-and-mahogany interior, loaded with a trunk CD changer and phone system. This was my one real luxury.

I tossed the keys to Stephanie and proceeded to find the security station. I got directions from a baggage clerk and headed that way.

The security office was on the lower level. Since the Olympics, the Atlanta airport is one of the most secure places in the state. When I entered the office, a pretty black female officer manning the desk was deep in a conversation on the phone, and it took her a couple of seconds to notice me standing there.

"Excuse me. My name is Noah Houston, and someone here paged me."

"If you wouldn't mind having a seat, someone will be with you in a minute, Mr. Houston," she replied, ending her conversation and hanging up the phone. As I turned in the direction of the available seats, she started whispering into a desktop voice module.

I wasn't seated ten seconds before a huge white man in a dark gray suit entered from one of the side doors. He stood at least six-eight and weighed close to three hundred pounds, with a marine cadet crew cut. He resembled a prehistoric man in an ill-fitted tailored European suit.

"Morning, Mr. Houston, my name is Detective Charles Harris, and I'm with Atlanta Homicide. Airport security has allowed me to use its office this morning, so do you mind coming in and having a seat. I have some questions for you," he said, pointing to the opened door.

"I'm sorry but what would a homicide detective want with me?" I asked incredulously.

"I'd like to speak with you in private if you don't mind."

"Well, I do mind! And I'm not going anywhere until you tell me right here and now what the hell is going on!"

"If you insist, Mr. Houston, we can do this here but I would have preferred to broach this subject in private," he continued with a tight smile working across his face. "I'm sorry to inform you, Mr. Houston, that your wife was murdered last night."

Chapter 3

"Will you come and have a seat in my office now, Mr. Houston?"

"Excuse me. Are you sure you have the right person? Are you sure it was Andrea? How did this happen?" I asked, feeling like this was all a nightmare and that I would wake up soon.

"I'll explain everything to you but first come this way," Detective Harris said as he grabbed me by the arm and guided me numbly into the office. I sat in the only other chair in the office. For the first time in my life, I felt an emptiness in my soul, and the tears started rolling down my face. Damn this hurt. But this can't be true, Andrea was the only woman I ever allowed myself to love, and now, according to this stranger, she's gone.

"Mr. Houston, can you hear me?"

"Yes, yes. Oh shit. Where is Ashley? Is she okay? Where is my daughter?"

"Calm down, Mr. Houston. I know I just dropped a bomb on you but for your daughter's sake you've got to pull yourself together. I'm sure you people should be used to having things like this happen to your immediate family and friends. Your daughter is fine, though. She was found in the house by one of our officers and taken to Emory Hospital for tests. Before we go any further, I have to ask you some questions if you think you're up to it, and I do still need you to identify the body."

"I don't understand what's going on here, and what do you mean by identifying the body? If I have to identify a body, how do you know it's really my wife, and what the hell do you mean by 'you people'?"

"Okay, Mr. Houston, let me give you all of the details before you say something you will regret. We received an anonymous call this morning from what we assumed was a professional contract killer. He informed us that he had just shot a woman, and there was a baby in the house, so we should send someone over to take care of it. I guess he's a hitman with a conscience. He didn't give us an address but he did leave his mobile phone for us to signal in on. We found your daughter still sleeping in her nursery, and, I'm sorry to say, your wife dead in your bedroom. We were not able to identify her from her physical appearance because of the gunshot wound to her head, but we were able to identify her from her driver's license fingerprint files."

"I still don't understand, why my wife?"

"Well, Mr. Houston, we were hoping you could provide us with some information, which would answer just that question. As I said before, we're one hundred percent certain this was a contract hit. Were you and your wife on good terms as far as your relationship was concerned?"

"Excuse me? You've just told me my wife was murdered, and you want to know if we were on good terms. Andrea is my wife, and we love each other dearly. What exactly are you trying to insinuate?"

"I am trying to be sensitive to your situation, Mr. Houston, but this was a contract hit. I can't tell you how many husbands have found it necessary to have their wives killed for a number of different reasons. Were you and your wife having problems, or are you involved with another woman?"

"I don't believe this! I'm just finding out that my wife was murdered and you're asking me if we had problems and who the hell else I'm fucking. I don't know what kind of husbands you're used to dealing with but I love my wife. I would do anything to bring her back, and I will do anything to find out who killed her. But let me make one thing perfectly clear, I did not or could not do anything that would jeopardize my wife or daughter."

Before Detective Harris could reply, the phone buzzed.

"Officer Jenkins, I asked not to be disturbed," Detective Harris barked into the receiver. He listened intently for a minute and hung up the phone defiantly.

"You seem to have company waiting for you, Mr. Houston. Would you like to tell me who the lady is that's threatening to call your lawyer? This wouldn't be your pretty white partner, would it? Are you sure there isn't something about her you would like to tell me now, before this gets ugly?"

I rose from my seat, realizing for the first time that tears were still flowing from my eyes. I looked at Detective Harris and said, "I have allowed you to abuse your position, which I will not do again. You will not close this case by accusing me of viciously killing the only woman I have ever loved. You will find the person who did this, so don't waste your time investigating my employees or me. If you aren't capable of finding my wife's killer, I can assure you I will, no matter what the cost. I'm going to get my child now. If you have a need for me I'm sure with the excellent detective skills you've shown so far you'll know how to reach me."

"This isn't a television show, Mr. Houston. I am investigating a vicious and according to you, senseless murder. Like it or not you are a suspect, no matter how much you profess to love your wife. So sit back down and tell me about your business."

Still standing I said, "I'm not telling you a damn thing. I told you before; you have no idea whom you're dealing with. I will give you this much though. You're right when you said this isn't television. If you're going to arrest me, do that. Read me my rights, file the charges, and let me call my lawyer. You can't intimidate me or get me to confess to something I couldn't or wouldn't do. It's your move now, because I'm going to go get my daughter."

"Before I let you go, Mr. Houston, let me leave you with a little information and a promise of my own. As far as we could see, there wasn't anything stolen. Very expensive trinkets were left around the house, so we're very confident that this was a contract hit on your wife and your wife only. Since you can give me no concrete reason why anyone else would want to hurt her, you are my number one suspect, so please don't leave this office thinking this is over. I've got a presidential suite waiting for you in our jailhouse."

Chapter 4

I don't make mistakes. I been good at this game for a long time. Completing contracts and killing people is as easy for me as masturbating. So I don't take kindly to killing the wrong person for free. I won't be pushed again to work a job at the last minute, fuck who wants it done. I can't believe that asshole had the nerve to want me to hit the right bitch the very next day. Chump didn't give a fuck about how hot the scene was. I told his stupid ass to go fuck himself. If I was going to do the job, it was going to be done my way. After a little hesitation, he realized I knew what the fuck I was talking about and left my ass alone to do what I do best.

I've been watching the bitch for about two weeks, and I can't wait to fuck her ass up. This sister is beautiful, fine, and hot.

The first sister I killed probably didn't know Ms. Thing but if she did she'd probably agree that they could pass for sisters. She looks about five-feet-seven-inches tall; long, black hair; and a milk-chocolate complexion. She's a perfect size eight with a tight round ass and healthy-looking, firm, tight tits. I missed out screwing the first one, but I definitely plan on laying some heavy pipe on this ho. She's single, no kids, and no security system installed that I could see. Her schedule has been pretty simple. She stays in most nights, during the day she shops, works out at the neighborhood tennis center, and does some kind of community work at Grady Hospital.

The house is a brick two-story colonial in a secluded cul-de-sac. It sits on a full acre by itself surrounded by trees on every side. I'm stationed about five hundred yards away from the house, deep in the trees. I been here since midnight watching. I don't plan on making any mistakes this time. As usual, she doesn't have any of her outside lights on. The last light on the inside she turned off about an hour ago. I love the fact that she's been so predictable. Every night she goes through the house and cuts off every light but the one in her bedroom before taking her ass to bed. She never goes straight to bed so I'm guessing she reads or plays with herself for about twenty to thirty minutes. I look at my watch and it's now 2:45 A.M., my time, pussy time. I hope it's as good as it's been looking.

It takes me a matter of seconds to cross the lot and get myself under the farthest window away from her bedroom. Scaling the wall isn't a problem. The window itself is locked. Looking through it, I don't see any sign of a motion detector or window alarms. Cutting the glass and unlocking the window goes without a hitch. I can barely control myself now. I take my nine out, even though I don't plan to use it for at least an hour and continue through the house. I can't believe how close I am to fucking this beauty.

After watching the house for these two weeks, I got a pretty good idea of how it's laid out. I assume this is a guest bedroom, since she's the only one living here. It has a king-size bed completely made, with a dresser and walk-in closet. This room leads to a hallway with a bathroom and another bedroom on the other side. At the end of the hall is her bedroom. The door is open, and it's dark as hell. My eyes adjust to the darkness, and I realize that my heart is pumping big time. I guess after watching this bitch as closely as I have, I can't wait to add that ass to my collection. I creep silently through the hall to the bedroom entrance. I can barely make out a form totally covered by the bed sheets in a huge king-size bed facing the entrance. I can't really tell how big the room is but I can make out a dresser, a StairMaster in the far corner, and a doorway to what I assume is the master bathroom. I put my nine back in its holster and pull out the switchblade. Barely controlling the smile that starts to creep across my face, I ease to the head of the bed.

"Looking for me, motherfucker?" a female voice whispers softly from the far right corner behind me. I turn around slowly and allow my eyes to adjust to the darkest part of the room. Standing next to a security monitoring system about twenty feet away with a gun pointed at me is the finest butt-naked sista I've ever seen. She moves a step toward me and before I can calculate what I have to do to throw this knife and disable her, a flash of light and explosion jumps from her hand. It takes me a second to realize that I am no longer standing.

"In case you haven't figured it out yet, I just shot your skinny ass. My baby 'Sig-Sauer' is loaded with hollow-point shells, and I don't think they're going to be able to replace that leg. The police should be here in about five minutes," she says emotionlessly.

"Bitch, I can't believe you shot me," I utter as I try to crawl across the carpet to her ass with one hand, while feeling for what was left of my leg with the other.

"Who the fuck you calling a bitch, you one-leg motherfucker? What did you expect when your ass came through my window? Another helpless mother that you could just destroy at your whim? I've been waiting for your ass for about two weeks. Had the motion detectors installed in every room once you started following me. I had them installed when you were watching me play tennis. I can't believe they sent such a shiftless little asshole after me anyway."

"I'm still going to kill your ass, bitch."

"Really," she said and another flash of light and thunder explodes from her hand and the pain in my other leg makes me cry out as I start to lose consciousness.

"Don't leave me now, baby. Be a man. Different on this end, isn't it? I owe you for killing that lady and making me miss two weeks of work. Do you have any idea how much money you're costing me? I promised myself that I would make your ass suffer for that shit. The least your stupid ass could've done in the beginning was to hit the right address. That lady died for nothing, and I hope she's waiting for your ass on your way to hell. Shit, I may let you live if you tell me who sent you and stop bleeding on my carpet. Can you hear me, little asshole?"

"Bitch, you don't have the guts to kill my ass."

"Damn, you're a dumb little motherfucker," she said. And the last light I was to ever see flashed from her hands.

Chapter 5

Why?

It's been weeks since I buried what was left of Andrea, and I still can't get past one question: Why would anyone want to kill her?

Ashley was released to me with a clean bill of health after Stephanie and I left the airport. I'm amazed at how hard my daughter is taking this. Even though Ashley's only nine months old, she seems to know her mother isn't around anymore. Ashley has been sleeping through the night almost from the time she was born, as well as being a quiet and playful child. Since she's been released from the hospital I can't get her to sleep more than one or two hours at most. She cries all the time, and since Andrea was breast-feeding her before she died, Ashley's having a difficult time adjusting to the bottle. I've taken her to the pediatrician, and the best advice she can give me is to bring her back home to her nursery and give her surroundings she's familiar with. I just haven't had the courage to go to the house.

I did hire a company to go in and clean the entire place as well as a carpenter to install a new front door to replace the one the police kicked in. Ashley and I have been living with my daddy and his wife since the funeral. I can't even bring myself to go home and pick up clothes for the both of us. I've been buying clothes and essentials as we need them. I know I can't do this forever but I just don't seem to have the strength to move back into the house, until today. I still feel the same way today but I realize this is something I've got to face, if not for me, at least for my daughter. In my mind, going back home and trying to put my life back on track would be a lot easier if I could just figure out why. Why did Andrea have to die? The police sure haven't gotten any closer to solving this case. The Atlanta detectives and district attorney have treated my family, employees, and me like suspected murderers. I can't believe they're spending as much time and energy as they are investigating me. I've let Stephanie take over most of the day-to-day business operations, and Detective Harris has called her in three times already just to question her personally. I just don't know when this will end.

Pulling into the driveway, I realize the house looks the same on the outside as it did before Andrea was murdered. I guess there's no way anyone would know by looking at the place that the most beautiful woman in the world was killed here.

The newspapers for the past three weeks have piled up on the doorstep, and the mailbox looks like it's going to burst. After opening the garage with the remote control and parking, I begin to compose myself mentally. As I reach for the door handle I realize I'm shaking, and I just can't do this. I start back outside and begin to pick up the newspapers and grab my mail. I sit on the trunk of my car and begin to sort through the mail. I realize I'm trying to postpone the inevitable for as long as possible.

Andrea and I loved this house. It was the first major purchase we made together. We had been house hunting for about six months, and collecting every item Andrea thought she just couldn't do without. The apartment was overflowing with black art, furniture, knickknacks, books, and baby items. Andrea loved picking up baby stuff even though she wasn't pregnant and we hadn't set a date for even trying to conceive a child.

Andrea called me on a windy November day so excited she could barely talk. "Noah, you've got to stop what you're doing and meet me in Stone Mountain. I know I've found the perfect house for us to spend the rest of our lives in."

"Baby, slow down. I thought we were looking for a starter home, something simple. Now you're talking about buying a house you want us to live in for the rest of our lives," I answered, slightly amused at the depth of her passion that she seemed to turn on and off at her whim.

"Don't you 'baby' me. I want this house. Now you get your ass out here, or I promise you, you'll be sleeping with your teddy bear for the next month," she exclaimed, barely controlling her laughter.

I met Andrea an hour later and immediately fell in love with the house, too. It's made of beautiful dark gray stucco, with large bedrooms and huge windows that circle the entire house. It's surrounded by a golf course on one side and tall pine trees on the other. The master bedroom has two huge walk-in closets as well as a Jacuzzi and a sunken tub with a separate shower. The basement is completely finished and carpeted. The original builder had filed for bankruptcy and was willing to sell the house well below the current market value.

The Realtor left us the keys and asked that we lock up after finishing our walk- through. She was late for her next showing, and I think she was very confident that Andrea was going to convince me that this was the house for us. We spent the next hour going through each and every room, imagining where the furniture and paintings would go, and the parties we would have. After an hour of dreaming we ended up making love on the floor in the middle of the master bedroom. How could I tell her no then? We signed the contract the next day.

I don't want to leave this house but I can't imagine staying here after what's happened. I've got to stop running and face this, I tell myself, and with that thought, I rise and proceed to open the front door.

The first sound I hear is the *beep-beep-beep* of the alarm system. Fine job it did the night Andrea was killed. She always felt like the system was a waste of money. It took a year before I could get her to set the alarm faithfully. I feel so stupid since it didn't help her in the end. After putting in the appropriate code and silencing the alarm I begin to feel totally drained. I take a seat on the steps leading upstairs to the bedrooms. It's amazing how the house smells so fresh and clean. I guess death doesn't leave an after smell. After a couple of minutes I stand and start surveying the house. I begin with the basement rooms and walk through the entire house. Everything is where I remembered it. Every painting and knick-knack is in its place, in the spots where Andrea had deemed necessary, as if the world depended on it. She had such a passion for each and every detail, like life itself revolved on everything being right where she put it.

I end up in front of our bedroom. The door is closed and for some reason I can't seem to get my hand to respond to my brain's command to open it. Before I can go any farther, the phone rings. I breathe a sigh of relief and run downstairs to answer it in the kitchen, never once thinking of going into the bedroom.

"Hello."

"Mr. Houston, this is Detective Harris."

"What can I do for you today? I'm busy, and I don't really have time for your questions."

"Well, I have some good news for you. Neither you nor your colleagues are suspects in your wife's murder anymore. The scumbag who killed her was killed this morning by another intended victim in the Hidden Hills area, and I must admit she did a damn good job of it!"

Chapter 6

It took me less than thirty minutes after hanging up to find myself in Detective Harris's downtown office.

"What do you mean you can't give me any details on the animal who killed my wife," I asked feeling angry and relieved at the same time. Angry, because I still had no idea who killed my wife or why. I felt relieved because I believed I would now be able to put some closure to this and find out why my wife was killed.

"Mr. Houston, I didn't say I couldn't give you details or any pertinent information regarding your wife's murder. I said I could not divulge the name of the young lady he attempted to kill yesterday. The investigation of the death of Charles Bradley, who we now know was a professional hitman is still ongoing. I'm under strict orders from my superiors to keep all information concealed. This animal may be responsible for a number of other crimes."

"I don't care what else the man did. I want to know why he killed my wife. You call and say that Andrea's murderer has been killed, and I'm no longer a suspect. Now you tell me he was a known hitman, but I'm not to worry. How do you know I didn't hire him myself?"

"You have a point, but there's other information you are not privy to that allows us to believe with quite a bit of certainty that you were not involved in the murder of your wife. We have items from his residence that connect him directly with your wife's murder as well as an attempt on another Hidden Hills resident who just happens to live at an address similar to yours. I shouldn't have told you the little that I have but I must admit we were sniffing up the wrong tree as far as you being a party to your wife's murder," Detective Harris continued.

"Is your half-ass apology supposed to make me feel better? I want to know who this man was, and since he's dead, how did it happen?"

"I really don't care if you accept what I have to say or not. This case is now closed, and you are no longer a suspect. My detectives and I have found your wife's killer who, as of yesterday, was killed himself. We have no proof that you were involved in the hiring of this contract killer. Case closed. You have a thriving business and a pretty little girl to raise now, so let us handle this. Go home, Mr. Houston."

"I've told you before, Detective Harris, you have no idea who you're dealing with. I'm not going anywhere until I get more answers. How would you feel if I called every newspaper and television station and put my little girl on the air? I'm sure the public would love to know what we have been going through and how the police department is concealing information for unknown reasons."

"I don't quite understand what information you're looking for to start off with, Mr. Houston."

"I want to know, who was this Bradley person? Who's the other woman he tried to kill and why? Why my wife?"

"Bradley has a sheet as long as your arm for everything from breaking and entering to rape and murder."

"And he was on the street?" I interrupted.

"All we can do is arrest them. Your weak-minded judges and equally weak-ass witnesses allowed Bradley to roam the streets. Actually it's been about four years since he was a guest in our hotel with bars. But, more often than not, a witness who claims to have been raped changes her story within two hours of identifying Bradley in a lineup. This guy had mucho juice, in and out of jail."

"None of this information tells me why he was after my wife."

"Again, Mr. Houston, I told you earlier we believe Bradley went to your house accidentally and killed your wife by mistake," Detective Harris continued sounding more and more bored and irritated with the conversation.

"You're contradicting yourself, how the hell could a so-called professional accidentally kill the wrong person?"

"What's your address, Mr. Houston?"

"1212 Terrace Green Trace," I answered agitated at the stupid question, which I knew he had an answer for.

"Do you have any idea how many Terrace Green streets are in Hidden Hills?"

"How the hell am I supposed to know that?" I demanded.

Reaching into his desk drawer, Detective Harris pulled out a detailed map of the Hidden Hills subdivision.

"There are approximately five other Terrace Greens. Terrace Green Trail, Terrace Green Lane, Terrace Green Drive,

GJT Simpson

Terrace Green Road, Terrace Green Circle. All of these streets have 1212 or 2121 address deviations. Bradley attempted to kill who we assume was the original victim yesterday morning. This lady's address is similar to yours. The difference is, she was ready for his ass, and it just didn't go the way he planned."

"What do you mean it 'didn't go as planned'?"

"She killed him. She shot off both of his legs and placed one square in the middle of his head. It's not often I get to see this kind of scum on the other end of the barrel. But you can rest easy knowing he died like a punk."

"Who is this woman? How did she know he was after her? Better still why was he after her?"

"I can't answer any of those questions, I've already told you more than I should have. Why can't you just let this go? As I said before, you have a beautiful little girl at home and a thriving business. Your wife's murder has been avenged, and her killer is dead. You're doing better than most of the cases I've had to deal with. You can go to bed tonight knowing he died as violently and painfully as he lived."

"What happened to the 'you people' you threw around so casually during our first meeting, Detective," I asked sarcastically. I recognized the fact that, at that moment I was just looking for someone to strike out at.

"I'm not sure I understand what you're talking about, but I do know this conversation is now over," Detective Harris replied as he got up from his seat and headed to the door, opening it slightly and pointing my way out.

"You're quite used to dismissing people at your whim as well as assuming we're all going to roll over when you say so, aren't you." I baited.

"Let me tell you something, Mr. Houston, I've been in this business for more than twenty years, and I can't believe how vicious these animals have become. I remember Atlanta when you could walk down any street, day or night, without looking over your shoulder. Nowadays the average citizen can't leave his or her house without wondering if it's the last time he's going to see his home again. It wasn't like this when we lived in Atlanta and ran Atlanta."

"Why use we, why not come out and say you white folks?"

"Read into it what you want, Mr. Houston, but facts are facts."

"Let me leave you with a couple of facts, Detective. Not forty or fifty years ago 'you people' beat, raped, and murdered us with total immunity. 'You people' have done everything in your power to keep us undereducated and unemployed. If 'you people' had your way, we would still be in the field picking cotton for free. 'You people' have spent the last three-hundred-plus years living freely off our sweat and tears, while 'we' played a major part in building this country into what it is. 'We' raised your kids, cleaned your asses, and wiped your noses. If some of our young people today are giving 'you people' grief, it's nothing compared to the grief 'you people' deserve. Whatever problems 'you people' are experiencing now, seems to have more to do with the lack of control that 'you people' are bred to believe is your God-given right. I do apologize for reality waking up and smacking 'you people' right in the face." With that statement and the stunned look still tattooed on his face I walked out of his office.

Chapter 7

I had no idea where I should start looking for answers, but before I did anything I needed to see Ashley. It took me about twenty minutes to get to my dad's house from the police station. My dad lives in a small single-story home next to Piedmont Park, which is located in the heart of Atlanta's midtown area. He has always liked this neighborhood because of the large old houses and beautiful oak trees that surround the park and its outlying areas. I've always thought the reason he likes this particular part of Atlanta was because it reminded him of New Orleans and the St. Charles Street neighborhood that he grew up in.

I let myself in and found him in his traditional spot, sitting in his recliner in front of the TV with Ashley fast asleep on his lap.

"Did you let me sleep on your lap as often as you've let Ashley?" I asked realizing that this is the first time I had smiled all day.

"You were a boy, and back in the old days, it wasn't quite right for a man to shower a boy with too much affection. I did love coming home after working on that riverfront all day and seeing your chubby little face grinning up from a bottle," He replied in his deep and hoarse-sounding voice. Pop tended to talk in a very slow and deliberate manner.

My father is a big man, but not necessarily in the physical sense. At five-foot- eight inches he wasn't what you would consider tall, but in my eyes he's big in every other way. Even at his age he has huge arms, a flat stomach, and a forty-six-inch chest. Pops been able to stay this way I guess from working twelve to fifteen hours a day with his hands and back for almost thirty-five years. He still works with his hands and back now that he's retired but as a landscaper.

Before he retired as a longshoreman, my dad was responsible for moving crates filled with everything from typewriters to grain out of the docked ships on the muddy Mississippi River in New Orleans. I will never forget how he would look coming home from work in those one-piece overalls, covered with sweat and dirt from head to toe. He usually fell asleep over his dinner before I had a chance to direct him to the bathroom and the tub filled with hot water and bubbles. As the only boy, it was my job to make sure he didn't fall asleep when he was supposed to be bathing. Pops would leave the biggest dirt ring in the world in the tub, and it would take every bit of strength my poor arms could muster to get it white again. Every Friday I would get a dollar allowance for cleaning his tub and baby-sitting him.

"I'm moving back into the house today," I announced while beginning to pack Ashley's bags.

"Are you sure that's what you want to do, boy? You know you're welcome to stay here as long as you want. I don't know why you're rushing this anyway. It's not often a man's wife is murdered in their own home," he said all the while gently rocking Ashley on his lap.

"I appreciate the offer, Pops, but I've got to face this now. By the way, that detective called this morning to tell me they found the guy who killed Andrea. Just so happens he was killed yesterday by another Hidden Hills resident."

"Who was he? How did he die? Did the cops get his ass?"

"Slow down, old man, one question at a time. The cops didn't have anything to do with killing him. From what little I was told, the woman he tried to kill killed him first."

"Damn, she sure got lucky. Who is she?"

"I don't know. There are a lot of unanswered questions, like why would a so-called professional hitman miss the first hit because of a wrong address and then allow himself to be killed by an intended victim. But, the number one question is who gave the orders for him to kill anyone to start off with?"

"I don't know, son, but I'm glad this is over now. You're going to have to get your life back to normal and concentrate on raising this pretty little girl," my father said patting Ashley gently on her back as he rose and placed her in the portable crib I had bought just for my dad's house.

"I realize that, Daddy, but it's not over for me yet. I have a lot of questions I want answered and I don't plan on resting until I get the answers I want," I said following him into the kitchen and picking up my baby's stuff along the way.

"Boy, have you lost your mind? You better let the police handle this. There ain't that much to handle anyway. I know you loved that girl, but she's dead. You can't change that. Why an animal like that would want to kill Andrea, I don't know. But, I do know this: She would want you to go on with your life and take care of this child of yours. Do you want some coffee, boy?" he asked, going to the cabinet and taking out a small coffee cup and saucer.

"No thanks, Dad. And you know you raised me to trust my gut feelings. As you like to say, 'Your gut won't steer a strong black man in the wrong direction.' My gut tells me there is something more to this than just a mistaken killing."

"Well, what about this child? I ain't going to let you run all over this city with this child under your arm. Why don't you let Jackie and me keep Ashley until you settle this?" he said as he prepared his coffee. My father has the weirdest coffee-drinking habit. He overflows this extremely small cup until the saucer itself has as much coffee on it as the cup. He then adds sugar and creamer to the cup. As he stirs it with a miniature silver spoon, it adds to the saucer's content. He then drinks from the cup until it's all gone and sips from the saucer. Now this is old school in every sense of the word since he explained to me years ago that this is a habit continued from his grandparents.

"I can't do that, Dad. I can't ask you or Jackie to do that. I'll manage somehow, I just need to sit and think this through."

"Boy, I'm ya daddy. I raised you to believe in family and the strength of the family. It's my job to help you when you need it, no matter how old and grown you are. Let my grandbaby stay with me until you get your head together and find some direction," he advised growling softly as he spoke the words.

I rose from my seat feeling uncomfortable with this conversation and walked back into the living room. I looked at Ashley's beautiful sleeping face and reached down into her crib and gently picked her up and laid her head gently against my shoulder while taking a seat on the sofa. "Pops, I'm barely keeping myself together emotionally. I never dreamed I would someday be without Andrea. You raised me all by yourself, and you've done a damn good job of it, but I've always missed having a mother. My child will have to replay my life all over again, because now her mother is dead, too. Her mother didn't die having my sister on some delivery table like my mother did, but because some animal took her life. Why? I can't just let this go. I'll let you keep Ashley for a few more days. I've missed too much time with her already, but I'm going to put the proper closure to this."

"Son, you know I'm not one for giving advice, but you've got to let this go. When your mother died, I grieved. I guess I grieved too long because I missed a lot of your childhood. I can never get that back, and I've spent my whole life trying to make up for that. Learn from my mistakes, you don't have to walk that walk."

"Pops, Moms died on the delivery table. There was nothing you could do about that. My wife was killed in our home, a home that we dreamed in and tried to raise a family in. I can't let this go. If you were in my shoes back in the day when you were trying to change the world without turning the other cheek, would you have walked away from this?" I asked.

"Don't put your mother in this, Noah. You know as well as I that there wasn't anything I wouldn't have done for her. Any man who would have had the heart to kill Mildred, on purpose or by mistake, would have died by my hands and my hands alone. But, Noah you know that was another time and place."

"I know that, Daddy. I'm not talking about killing anybody, and you know I don't believe in guns, even though I know how to use one. I still owe you for teaching me how to fight with my hands. But, I'm talking about finding the man who started this nightmare and bringing him to justice, legal justice in our courts. I need your help and support. Take care of Ashley for me for a few days. If I can't bring this to a close by then, I give you my word as your son, I'll put this to rest."

"I love you, Noah. You my boy. I'll take you at your word, and two weeks from now I expect you to come to my house whole again and ready to take on the responsibility of being a father and a son, you understand?"

"I hear you, Dad, but I don't know if I will ever be whole again."

"I know how you feel. As you youngsters say been there, done that," Pops said with a knowing smile that I realized I needed to see. "Have you been working out at all lately?" he asked.

"No, old man. I've just been too caught up in this to do myself any good, but I do plan on airing out the basement and getting back to it. My body feels like it's a hundred years old."

"Well you betta get back on it, and changing the subject, have you seen the ad I put in your Hidden Hills newspaper for my lawn service?"

I can't tell you the last time an idea hit me so fast and so hard as it did at the exact moment I realized what my father had just asked. It's like a door had been flung opened and the brightest light imaginable had hit me dead in the face.

"No, I haven't, Pops, but you've just given me a great idea."

While Pops was sitting there with his mouth wide open I kissed Ashley and gave her a big hug. Telling Ashley good-bye and giving her to Pops, I headed out of the door, feeling a sure sense of direction for the first time since this nightmare began.

Chapter 8

As soon as I got home, I started going through the mail I had collected earlier. I was looking for a name. A name that Andrea had mentioned a couple of times when we first moved into the subdivision. I think her name was Claudia, and I do remember that she was the editor of our community subdivision newsletter *The Hidden Hills Gazette*.

Claudia was known for her unrelenting desire to keep Hidden Hills a crime-and-drug-free community, as well as her unquenchable appetite for gossip. I remember Andrea telling me how she showed up a week after we moved in bearing housewarming gifts and digging for information. Not many people can attest to being as patient or understanding as Andrea was, but by the time I got home she was literally fuming. According to Andrea, the conversation started off pleasantly but quickly turned nasty.

Apparently Claudia had decided that she was going to do everything in her power to screen each and every resident in Hidden Hills and dissuade the undesirables from continuing to live here. She wanted to know if we were married or just living together. Where had we lived prior to moving here? What did we do for a living? Did we have intentions of raising a family? How many kids did we have? What were our religious affiliations? Did we smoke or drink? And about thirty other questions that seemed increasingly more personal. Andrea said she finally got tired of being the pleasant hostess and told her that she had a lunch engagement and would talk to her at another time. Claudia didn't like that and left in a huff. Andrea never heard from her directly again, but she did see her at all of the monthly association meetings. Claudia usually spoke briefly to Andrea while walking away with her nose stuck in the air.

Bingo! The newsletter was on the bottom half of my unopened mail. *Claudia Fisher, Editor* was lavishly displayed across the top of the paper, taking up almost as much space as the paper name. I quickly scanned the paper for the office number and started to give her a call. I was in such a rush when I first got in I had completely forgotten about my prior uneasiness with the house and the fact that the message light on the answering machine was blinking. Ignoring the light I proceeded to call Claudia, and in turn got a busy signal. After hanging up the phone, I listened to the messages. The only one of any importance was from Stephanie with an urgent message for me to call the office.

Calling Stephanie made me realize how much my life had changed with the murder of my wife. I didn't had the heart to step into the office since this tragedy happened, let alone put together a string of thoughts for any major business decisions. I couldn't tell you the last time I went weeks without my cell phone and pager. As I start to call Stephanie, I realize that I didn't know where I last laid my "electronic connections to the world." Being this vulnerable for this long had truly changed my opinion of myself and my prior sense of strength and control. If someone had told me a couple of months ago that I would walk away from my business in the middle of the biggest contract in our brief history and allow someone else to assume control of the day-to-day operations, I would have laughed in his face. But, how do you prepare for the death of a loved one? How do you strengthen yourself for the day you wake up and the person you have spent almost your entire adult life with is taken from you? I wonder if I'll ever let myself be in this kind of situation again, knowing what I know now.

"Good afternoon, HSD, Inc. How may I direct your call?" Mary's happy voice answered.

"Good afternoon, Mary. Have you and the crew burned down the office yet?" I asked trying to muster up as much genuine humor as possible. Mary is our college intern who helps answer the phones when we are busy and shorthanded.

"Mr. H! It's so good to hear from you. We miss you, and I'm not just saying that either," she said with just a touch of sadness in her voice. Mary always called me Mr. H, even though she knows I would rather she call me Noah. Her reasoning has always been that her mother raised her to address her elders and employers as Mr. or Mrs. I told her that calling me Mr. Houston made me feel like an old man, so she came up with Mr. H instead. "Are you coming back to work soon?"

"I'm afraid not, Mary. I'll be out for at least a couple more weeks. I appreciated the flowers you and the staff sent, and it meant a lot to me to see you at the funeral." Saying this, I began to wonder if there would ever be a time when my chest wouldn't hurt when talking about Andrea's death.

"Don't worry about it, Mr. H. I'm just so sorry that something like this had to happen to your wife. She was always so nice and polite to me whenever she called."

"Thanks, Mary. Is Stephanie in?"

"Sure, she's been waiting for your call. Hold on, and I'll put you through."

It was only moments before Stephanie picked up.

"Are you sitting down, Noah?" Stephanie almost shouted into the phone.

"Calm down, lady. Should I be sitting down? I'm not sure I can take anymore bad news in this lifetime."

"No, it isn't bad news," she responded, realizing she was a little bit out of control. "And I guess I shouldn't have approached it this way, but we're so excited here."

"All right then, tell me the good news so I can feel better, too."

"We got the contract this morning. They sent it here via Fed-Ex. All we need now is your John Hancock. I've looked over the numbers and time schedule. Everything is just the way you wanted it."

"Great news, Stephanie. This wouldn't have happened without you. I'm well aware of how much time and energy you've spent keeping the business afloat the last few weeks."

"Well that's what you've been grooming me for since day one, isn't it?" Stephanie answered, sounding a little sad.

"I'm glad you finally realize that, and now I need you more than ever. I've got a lead on who killed my wife, and I need you to keep the business going. You know about the design, development, and implementation of the project as well as our predetermined time lines. Take the ball and run with it. I'll just be a phone call away if there are any problems. The way I look at this, I'll have put some closure to this within the next few weeks at the most."

"You're the boss, and you know I will do anything to help you and this business. Take whatever time you need to heal. Do me a favor though, remember that this is your baby, and I can only provide a temporary nursery. The company and I need your leadership and fire."

"Point taken. Have the courier drop off the papers at my dad's house, and I'll sign them and make the appropriate follow-up calls so we can get this ball rolling. Remember, I'm only a phone call away."

"Okay, boss. I'll send the papers and talk to you later."

I called Claudia's number again and was able to get through this time. She sounded exactly as I had imagined from Andrea's description. Her voice was very high-pitched.

"Mr. Houston, what can I do for you?" she asked after I had introduced myself.

"I'd appreciate it if you would call me Noah, Claudia."

"That being the case, Mr. Houston, I would rather you address me as Mrs. Fisher. Now what can I do for you?" she answered, forcing me to remember that I needed her help, not the other way around.

"I'll get to the point, Mrs. Fisher. I heard there was another attempted break-in at one of the houses in our subdivision, which resulted in the perpetrator being killed. Have you heard anything about the incident?"

"Do I look like the local newspaper to you, sir?"

"I'm sorry, Mrs. Fisher. Did I just catch you at a bad time or are you always this witchy?" I replied, fully aware that no matter how badly I needed this information, there was no way I was going to accept this abuse from anyone.

"I wasn't surprised to hear about your wife, given her inability to grasp the seriousness of our personal safety, but at least now after talking to you, I can tell it must be a family defect," she said in a huff.

As I listened to her, I realized that it was time for me to cut my losses and figure out another way to find this mystery lady. My patience had diminished tenfold since this conversation started, and I was afraid I was going to spit out all of the bitterness that has been locked in me since Andrea's death on this narrow-minded ignorant lady. As I started to hang up the phone, she continued her verbal assault.

"Your wife was probably just as bad as that tramp who killed that trash last week. I never thought I would see the day when a Cascade Road stripper would move into our neighborhood. I wonder how your wife would feel if she knew one of those Club Amazon tramps was living within a stone's throw of her and her child. But she had no trouble condemning me because I insisted we screen each and every new home owner so this unpleasantness would not happen. Your wife shouldn't have had to die and leave that beautiful child here alone. That tramp wasn't worth it."

It took all of the patience I could muster, but after five minutes more of her continuous ranting, I had all of the information I needed.

Chapter 9

Death is difficult. In my thirty years on this earth, with the exception of my mother, I've never had anyone close to me die. I've had friends of friends who died, and I listened to them cry and reminisce, but still no one I was close to. Growing up I often thought of how my mother had died on that delivery table bringing my sister into this world. I still wonder about how different my life would have been with my mother at my side. I think about all of the memories we didn't get to share and the life experiences my daughter won't have now that her mother is gone. Two generations growing up without the love and memories of their mother. My dad did a hell of a job with me, but I was a little boy. He understood me. I'm not in the same situation since I've got a little girl to raise. How am I going to teach her all of the things I know absolutely nothing about? I don't know how to comb hair or buy a dress, much less how to talk to her about boys and relationships when that time comes. This is not the way our lives were supposed to be. Damn, this hurts!

Everything in my life is so different now. I know how death feels. It's a hurt I can't come close to explaining. I miss Andrea so much. Everywhere I go, everything I touch, every thought I think is attached to her in one way or another. I wake up in the middle of the night after dreaming of the many moments we spent together loving, planning, playing, and arguing. Death forces you to appreciate and miss the bad times as well as the good times. There were very few bad times with Andrea, but her temper was legendary. Just thinking about Andrea's temper brings an unannounced smile to my face through the tears. Boy could she argue. Once she made up her mind she was right about anything, no matter how trivial, she wouldn't let it go. I'll never forget our first major argument after we were married and had moved into the house. I was putting together a proposal for a major client during HSD's first year. I left for work about four that morning, hoping to get a head start and put a new idea on paper before I lost the concept when my cell phone started ringing. It was Andrea. She had gotten up to use the bathroom and wanted to know why I hadn't put my toothbrush back in the holder after using it. I started laughing and told her to go back to bed, that I would talk to her later and hung up the phone.

Thirty seconds later she was calling again. "Noah, I don't understand why it's so hard for you to do the simple things," she started, her voice getting louder and louder. "I know you have a lot of things on your mind, but it's so simple to just put the toothbrush right where you got it from."

"Andrea, go back to bed. I'm sure you will find more earth-shattering things to fuss about after the sun comes up," I replied testily and with that said I hung up the phone and turned off the power so that I didn't have to continue with this drama. When I finally got to my desk after spending the last ten minutes of the drive stewing over Andrea and her moods, I had barely sat down when my desk phone rang. I knew it was Andrea, but I answered it anyway.

"What do you want, Andrea?" I asked barely concealing the disdain in my voice.

"On your way home today, you need to buy another toothbrush. The one you left on the sink accidentally fell in the toilet." I didn't get a chance to reply before she hung up.

I thought seriously about calling her back, but then I realized I was fighting a no-win battle. If I called we would spend the whole day arguing about something I didn't even care about. I could also go home at lunch, take Andrea by the hand and walk her through the house, starting at the front door and point out the dress shoes she took off two days ago while eating dinner, still under the dining room table her bathrobe thrown across the sofa from that morning, not to mention the dishes. We've had a working dishwasher since the first day we moved in the house. This fact didn't keep her from running a sink full of water and soaking the dishes, glasses and pots for days at a time. There's nothing like coming home after working twelve hours, to prepare a simple meal and have a kitchen with three days worth of stacked, crusty, and smelly dishes staring at you. This, from a woman who would call me at four o'clock in the morning crying because I didn't put my toothbrush in the holder.

Andrea always brought to mind a friend of my father's when describing his feelings for his wife of forty years. "I've loved her always but there are times that my 'like' for her is greatly exhausted."

I can't explain my emptiness. I miss her so much.

Chapter 10

I awoke the next morning after another restless night, with an idea that I thought just might work. My plan couldn't go into effect until dusk so I decided to direct my energies toward something more concrete. I called Pops first to check on Ashley and to find out what things they would need for the next couple of weeks. The list was small since he and Jackie had gone grocery shopping the night before.

My dad met Jackie after I left for college. They had been acquaintances since high school and had begun dating after my mother's death. Jackie's a pretty lady, small in stature and quiet. She pampers my father as much as he'll let her, but she always seems to withdraw whenever anyone else is around. I've never been very close to her but I'm glad Pops has her in his life. I don't think there's a thing she wouldn't do for him.

Quiet as she is, there have been many a moment she's left us speechless and proud to have her as a part of the family. She surprised us all when she showed up at the hospital with Pops when Ashley was born. When they arrived, Andrea was having a hard time getting Ashley to begin breast-feeding. No matter what the nurses or Andrea tried, they couldn't get Ashley to suckle. Andrea was starting to freak out, and there was nothing I could do to help the situation. We were totally blown away when Jackie took Ashley in her arms and started to sway while softly singing one of the sweetest songs I had ever heard. Still singing, she laid Ashley next to Andrea and gently brushed Ashley's tiny mouth against Andrea's breast. Within seconds Ashley had moved her little hands to encircle her mother's breast and began to nurse. We could never figure out why this worked for Jackie and not for anyone else. Maybe it was the quiet peace that seemed to encircle the room once Jackie started singing. Jackie stayed at the hospital for the next two days helping Andrea and Ashley become comfortable with each other. For this and the love she shares with my pop, I will always be grateful.

My next move was to track down Charles, an old college roommate who worked for me when I first started the business. Charles has always been a carefree and strange breed. During college he was the class organizer, especially if it had something to do with women and partying. If you wanted to know where the happenings were and who was going to be there, Charles was the person to ask. He graduated a year after I did, but ended up working as a telemarketer for about seven bucks an hour.

I ran into Charles in the mall about two years after graduation. We ended up eating lunch, and he convinced me that I needed to put him in charge of sales if my organization was ever going to be truly successful. The fact that he knew absolutely nothing about computers or the industry didn't seem to dampen his belief that he knew exactly how to increase our sales by fifty percent in one year. He did have a couple of stipulations: He needed three thousand dollars a month salary plus ten percent of all new sales profits and a month paid in advance, due to some financial problems at the time. To this day, I can't explain why I gave Charles a job and the money upfront, but I did. He wasn't happy about the "no" he got as far as the ten percent profit-sharing idea was concerned but he did go on to increase our sales by one hundred percent the first three years, making more money personally than he had ever made previously.

Charles worked hard, learning the business and using his carefree personality to meet new contacts and promote the company. We worked well together for a number of years until the nightlife started to get the best of him. Charles still felt that he could party all evening, come to work the next morning directly from some nightclub and function as normal. His favorite clubs were the black strip joints that seemed to pop up and disappear every other month. He finally got so burned out that he asked me to grant him a leave of absence for about three months so that he could refocus his energies and realign his goals.

I knew he would never come back the moment he left the office, but I have always believed that as an adult we have to walk the walk we choose for ourselves. He sent the office a bouquet of flowers and a couple of boxes of candy about two months into his self-imposed hiatus. He also sent a personal note to me explaining that he really appreciated the break that I provided but he felt he was doing the company and our friendship more harm than good, and with that he resigned. He still dropped in at the office every month or so just to tell me about his newest female conquest. He was a pallbearer at Andrea's funeral and worked on a couple of deals Stephanie wasn't able to get to during my preparation for the funeral. I guess the saying is true that you never know who your true friends are until adversity strikes.

Since it was close to nine o'clock I figured Charles would just be walking in from clubbing, and I wanted to talk to him before he fell asleep. He answered the phone on the first ring.

"What's up, player? You sleep yet?" I asked.

"You the player, man, but the question should be how the hell are you and Ashley? I still can't get over what happened to Andrea. Y'all hanging right?" Charles asked.

"I guess as well as can be expected given the situation. Ashley is staying with my dad for a minute while I take care of some business that I need your expertise on."

"Cool, whatcha need, my brother?"

"I need some information on the Amazon's Dinner Club, and I know you're the man when it comes to the tittie joints," I replied, anticipating and getting the shocked response that I expected.

"What the hell you want to know about Amazon's. You ain't been to a strip club since college. I know you in pain right now man, but ain't shit in Amazon's for you!" he exclaimed barely keeping his voice from cracking.

"Man, chill out. I'm not going to Amazon's looking for a woman, per se. To tell you the truth, I am looking for a woman, but it's because I'm trying to find out who killed Andrea."

"I saw on the news that they found the piece of shit who killed her and that he's dead now," Charles replied, sounding more and more bewildered.

"Yeah, he's dead but this is far from over. I'm going to find out who's responsible for my wife's murder, and I'm not going to stop at some second-level flunky. I can't go into the full story now but I have a lead, and it points to a stripper who works at Amazon's. Have you been there lately?"

"Just last week, but it's not like you, and I remember when we used to go in college. Most of the women there now are more street than strippers. They all seem to have their hair weave, fake nails, gold teeth, and tattoos over half of their bodies. You give them a dollar, and they'll do damn near anything."

"Well, the one I'm looking for doesn't fit that mold. I've been told that she looks a lot like Andrea."

"I didn't see anyone like that when I was there, but it wasn't a weekend either. All of the strippers I know work on the weekends, no matter how many days they work during the week. It's all about making money, and the weekends are prime-time money time."

"So you think she'll be there tonight?" I asked realizing that it was Friday. Since this drama began I'd had a hard time keeping track of the hours, much less the days.

"Like I said 'prime-time money time.' If she's a true stripper, tonight's the night. Most folks still get paid on Fridays, and some of our brothers still like giving away the loot as quickly as possible."

"Thanks, my brother, you've helped me out a lot. I'll give you a call later on if I need anymore information. By the way, who's running the club now?"

"Some high-yella nigga named Dominique Lawson, supposedly owns the club but the rumor is he's just a black-paper front man for the mob or something. You know as well as I do, that that particular rumor's been going on since we were kids."

"Yeah, well it doesn't really matter anyway. I'm not going there to bring the place down. I just need some questions answered."

"Well, call me if you need anything else. You know you still my nigga, and there ain't a damn thing I wouldn't do for you. Except maybe staying out of the nightclubs," he said with a smile I could hear over the phone.

"Later, man. Keep it straight," I said, smiling as I hung up.

I changed into my workout sweats and started to the only part of this big old house that was truly mine, the basement and my workout room. None of Andrea's feminine touches had made their way to this section. We agreed early on that I wouldn't give her any grief as far as the interior decorating of the upstairs if she would leave the basement to my "masculine pursuits."

I had mirrors installed on every wall, with huge ceiling fans providing the only real air conditioning. A fourth of the floor is covered with four-inch-thick tumbling mats, and in the center of the mats is a boxing bag hanging from the ceiling. Against the wall I have a state-of-the-art StairMaster and treadmill. Jump ropes, boxing gloves, and a thousand pounds of free weights and bars cover the other side. A forty-inch television with cable and a stereo system completed the room. This was my place, my hideaway when it was too cold or rainy to play tennis, or I just didn't want to be bothered. It was here that I came to practice the art of survival that my father taught me and I in turn wanted to pass on to my son, a son I wanted to have with Andrea.

After one of the many fights I had when I first entered junior high, my father came home to find Mrs. Johnson cleaning up the bruises left on my head by the current resident school bully. Mrs. Johnson was the closest thing that Gina and I had to a mom when we were younger. She and her husband lived just down the block, and she would come over every day to cook our meals, clean the house, make sure we were ready for school the next morning and spank our butts when we needed it. When my father came home and asked what happened, I really didn't know how to tell him that I was getting my butt whipped, so I told him I fell running at school. He gave me one of those, I'm-your-daddy-and-I-know-you're-lying looks and told me to follow him outside to the backyard.

He sat on the grass and told me to do the same.

"Now, boy, you know I don't take to you lying to me, so tell me what the hell is going on!" he said in his barely audible voice.

"Dad, it ain't nuthin' I can't handle. One of the guys at school is just giving me a hard time, that's all," I replied, trying to end the conversation as quickly as I could.

"Can ya fight, boy?"

"Daddy, that's silly, 'course I can fight."

"Alright then, stand up and fight me," he said, rising slowly.

I jumped up immediately and started to prance around like I had seen the fighters do on TV. "Okay, but don't be mad if I hurt you, old man."

The last word had barely left my mouth when I felt a sharp pain in the middle of my stomach and a bright light went off in my head. The next thing I remembered was the sweet smell of grass and the way it tickled my face. I opened my eyes, and I was lying smack in the middle of the yard with my dad stretched out next to me calmly smoking a cigarette.

"What happened?" I mumbled, struggling to sit up.

"While you were looking pretty bouncing around, I hit you in your stomach," he said with a faint smile.

"That's not fair, Daddy. I didn't tell you I was ready. It's bad enough you're bigger than I am, you didn't have to sucker-punch me," I said angrily as the tears rolled down my face.

"Boy, any time you raise your fists or speak to a man in a challenging way ya betta be ready to fight. And rule number one when it comes to fighting is there are no rules," he continued as he wiped the tears from my eyes. "Let me ask you this, boy. Why are you fighting to start off with?"

"I don't want to fight, Daddy. It's just that people seem to just want to pick on me all the time. I tried walking away but the kids still chase me and want to fight me."

"You still didn't answer my question, boy. I didn't ask you why they're fighting you, I asked why are you fighting," he said, sounding more and more disgusted with me.

"I'm fighting to make them leave me alone."

"And you think that just because you fight them they're going to leave you alone, boy?"

"Yeah. What else am I going to do?"

"Do you want to fight me again?"

"Hell no. That hurt," I said, knowing I had no business cursing in front of my dad.

"Do you ever think about hurting the kids who try to hurt you?"

"Not really. I just want it to stop once it starts."

"I never want to interfere with you becoming a man, but I won't let anyone hurt you, including yourself. I think you're old enough and mature enough for me to start teaching you the physical and mental tools to win, when you have to fight.

"Always remember, a man never picks a fight. I only fought to defend my family or myself. Do you understand this?"

"Yeah, but why would I want to start a fight anyway?" I asked, not understanding how he could think that I would start a fight for no reason.

"The things I can teach you about fighting, I learned as a Panther. These were the skills that kept us alive, but I also saw some guys use these tricks to become big bullies on the street. I won't allow that to happen to you. I show you how to defend yourself, and I betta never catch you picking on anybody, ya hear me?"

"I hear ya, Dad. I just don't want to get my butt whipped again."

"Okay, but answer me this. Where do you think a fight is won or lost?" he asked.

"Oh, that's easy, with your fists. If I could hit harder than the other guy, I can win," I replied.

"Wrong. The fight any fight, be it in a schoolyard or boardroom, starts in ya mind," he said, pointing to his head. "Ya have to be at peace in your mind. Ya have to know you are willing and ready to do anything to win and end a fight as quickly as possible. Because there are no rules once a fight begins but to survive with as little effort and pain as possible."

With that, my weekly training began. My father taught me many techniques about survival over the next few years, a number of which I've taken from the street to the boardroom. He taught me how to walk into a room looking and feeling confident. He was a firm believer that people only picked on those who looked and acted vulnerable. There was the breathing and stretching exercises that helped me to relax and allow my mind to be conscious of my surroundings at all times. And of course there were the fighting skills. My father had combined many of the styles he had seen and been a part of into his own art. It was a combination of boxing, judo, karate, and street fighting, the likes of which I had never seen.

I've spent many hours honing this ability but have had very few reasons to use it. I may have had one more fight in school after my daddy started working with me and that one didn't last long. The same bully who had battered and bruised me on the day this all started tried to pick a fight with me about three weeks later. As soon as he walked up to me I knew there was going to be a fight. He started to talk trash trying to get everyone's attention so that he could prove again how big and bad he was at my expense. This time I didn't wait. I looked him straight in the eyes and kicked him as hard as I possibly could between his legs. He immediately screamed and crumpled to the ground in a fetal position. Everyone around us was in shock. Then I leaned over him and told him if he ever so much as looked in my direction again I would break his little neck, and with that my reputation was born.

I worked out hard for a little more than two hours trying to make up for all of the time I had missed. I spent about forty-five minutes on the StairMaster and another thirty minutes on the bicycle in front of the TV. Twenty minutes on the speed bag and another ten minutes on the heavy bag totally wore me out. I spent another thirty minutes stretching and practicing kicks and striking routines. After showering and cooking dinner, I sat at the computer for about three more hours answering e-mail and paying bills. Then I lay down in bed knowing I would need to be totally rested for the long night ahead. Nightclubs in Atlanta don't start humming till about midnight, and I didn't want to miss a thing.

Chapter 11

I was dressed and on the road by 11:30. Amazon's was located in the heart of Atlanta in the black red-light district. Atlanta, for all of the leadership it provided during the sixties civil rights movement still has two very distinctly different worlds for whites and blacks. Neighborhoods in Atlanta are now sixty percent black, and in some of the more destitute areas are close to ninety-nine percent black. Inner city "white flight" from the so-called fear of shrinking property values and a rise in crime when blacks move in to their neighborhoods has changed the overall Atlanta landscape. This white flight has had its positives as well as its negatives. Many black folks, including Andrea and I, have been able to take advantage of this uncalled for fear. We are now able to purchase houses and businesses in these previously exclusive neighborhoods for a fraction of what the original owners had invested in them. I've personally never seen any kind of shrinking property value in the newly predominantly black neighborhoods.

I've experienced the exact opposite for our house whose overall value has increased. A couple of my friends have seen larger business profits from businesses they bought for pennies on the dollar from whites in a rush to leave as the neighborhoods started to change to a darker complected clientele.

That's the positive aspect but there's also a darker more sinister response. Many of our neighborhoods have bars and liquor stores, two or three to a block, with fast-food restaurants and abandoned buildings scattered throughout. Meshed within are numerous nightclubs and strip joints that pop up and change owners as often as the seasons. White folks will picket businesses and change zoning codes if too many fast-food restaurants start to pop up. You mention opening up a bar or a strip joint, and you're likely to have a mysterious fire at the business late one night. Whatever happened to good old American capitalism?

Amazon's is located in this kind of a neighborhood. Situated in the middle of the block, it is a gray single-story structure fenced in completely with a huge neon sign promoting live nude female boxing every Wednesday night. There were cars parked haphazardly inside of the fence. You could get your car parked in the VIP section, which was in the very front of the club. Most of the cars parked there were Cadillacs, Mercedes, BMWs, and the custom-refinished classics. The classic low riders had drop-top hoods, custom ragtops, and were souped up with hydraulic pistons that allowed the driver to make the car dance. I've seen some of the cars rolling on just the rear wheels, as well as on just the wheels on one side of the car. The hydraulic systems also allowed them to jump and bounce from a standing position.

It took me about five minutes to find an open space on the far side of the building, close to the entrance/exit gate, but underneath one of the better-lighted areas. As I got out of the car and started for the door, one of the street valets eyed me and started in my direction.

"Yo, my nigga. Ya sure ya don't want to pay an extra ten and park where we can take care of ya ride in our valet spots. Driving a cold-ass ride like that I know ya got the Benjamins for the special treatment," he said as his other boys looked on.

My valet couldn't have been more than fourteen. He was tall and lanky, with a mouth full of gold teeth and about ten gold chains around his neck. He walked with a visible limp and seemed to have a hard time walking a straight line. He had on jeans, a hundred-dollar pair of Nikes, and an Amazon's T-shirt. The shirt had a picture of about six fully naked sisters bending over showing all of their assets. In bold print across the top was *"Amazon's - Only Freaks Need Apply for Freaknik 2001!"*

"No thanks, my young brother. I've got protection," I replied as I turned around and hit my car key button, which set the alarm and signaled it with two quick horn bursts. "But there is something else you can do for me." I reached into my pocket and peeled off a twenty-dollar bill from a roll I had prepared for show, just for tonight.

"I want you to watch my car personally, plus give me some info on a dancer I think may be working tonight," I said while putting the rest of my money back into my pocket and turning the twenty I had taken off the roll over and over in my hands.

"What kind of info ya need, man, cuz ya know I the nigga with the juice. I can set ya up with a sister if ya looking for some no-work pussy. You don't even have to go in there," he said, pointing to the door of the club and grinning broadly.

"That's all right, little man. I need to see some new sights, if you know what I mean," I said, grinning back at him, working on making him feel comfortable with me. The whole time this was going on, his boys were watching him, and he couldn't take his eyes off the twenty.

"I unnerstan'. I guess everybody git tired of looking at that old wife every day," he said, laughing at his own sense of humor.

"Yea, ya got that right. You're pretty bright for a youngster. What's your name?"

"They call me Crip, cuz I got a little stutter to my shake," he replied, demonstrating his walk in case I didn't get it when he first came up.

"Crip, I'm looking for a certain lady that's supposed to dance here. I don't know her name but the way she was described to me was a tall, dark-skinned, pretty lady. Looks like she could take on the world if she had to."

"Say no mo', my nigga. I know the bitch ya talking about. She a real bitch, too. I don't know why ya wanna go and mess with that stuck-up ho anyway. She walk around here wit her nose stuck up in the air, make me want to trip that bitch just to see her come off that high hill she on. That bitch wouldn't even touch her toes fo' ya and show that stuff, so don't be wastin' yo' time wit her ass. I gots me some bitches that'll take ya around the world for twenty bucks, and they look twice as good as that ho," he said with disgust written on his face.

"It's all good, my brother. I just have a special taste for the lady. Do you know if she's here tonight?"

"Bitch here every Friday and Saturday. Stealing niggas' money. If they knew that ho wasn't going to give up a damn thing, they wouldn't waste so much loot on her ass. But by the time they realize ain't shit going on but that ho's rent getting paid, most of they dumb asses broke."

"Thanks for the heads up, my man, I'll try to keep most of my money in my pocket." And with that I handed him the twenty.

As soon as the bill touched his hand, he seemed to forget about all the hatred he was working on and a smile raced across his face.

"I'll take good care of ya ride, man, an' don't forget I got some good special pussy waitin' on you when ya ready."

I turned and walked toward the door, knowing that the only thing protecting my car was the alarm installed in it, but the twenty got me some info I could use.

The front of the building had a number of tables set up with T-shirts, jeans, hats, and other things you may need to buy at midnight for a little less than you would pay at a store as long as you didn't ask for a receipt. You couldn't get in without being offered a wide variety of products. There was one table with a TV/VCR setup selling bootleg movies that were still in theatres. These guys were selling them for twenty-five dollars a movie unless you bought two or more, which dropped the price down to twenty dollars each. They also sold triple X-rated movies, which one of the guys said he had in the back of his car because he didn't want "five-o" to put him in jail. I guess selling bootleg movies wasn't enough for the cops in Atlanta to bust you for these days.

I walked past the gray steel door to a window on my right where a woman about fifty years old told me that the cover charge was twenty dollars. She took my twenty, handed me a ticket, and pointed me through the two metal detectors to my left. I walked through both of the detectors without them going off but was still met by a huge bouncer before I was allowed to enter the dark club.

"Yo, man, I need to pat ya down," he said with one of the most effeminate voices I had ever heard coming from a six-feet-eight-inch black man. After patting me down, he directed me through another set of twin doors.

Entering the club was like waking up on another planet. The first thing I noticed was the partially and completely naked women in every direction I looked. There had to be at least fifty women of every shape, shade, and deviation of black known to man. There was also a couple of white and Asian sisters. Most were sitting or standing around the bar, which was a circular area built right in the middle of the club. Coming off four different points were thirty-foot runways that each ended at a five-by-five square. Each runway had metal poles that ran from the ceiling to the floor in the small dance area. Music blared from huge fifteen feet speakers that were suspended by metal cables in every corner. The deejay stood in a glass-enclosed booth suspended above the far wall. I couldn't see into the deejay booth, but I could make out two silhouettes, one male and the other a perfectly formed female. The deejay was playing Tupac's "All Eyez On Me," and it seemed like every table was occupied as well as every runway. One naked dancer had climbed to the top of one of the poles and was hanging facedown from the ceiling and holding on by squeezing her naked thighs tightly around the pole. Her blond hair flowed across the stage as she tried to hold her breasts up as the ten guys surrounding her tossed money that she attempted to catch with her mouth.

There were small booths lining each of the four walls. The booths had no lights in them but you could make out a table and cushioned seats built into the walls. Dancers occupied the majority of the rooms in various stages of nakedness with their clients. Some of the booths were filled with just dancers as they sat with their shoes off, smoking, drinking, and checking out the clients for an easy pick.

I took a seat at the farthest end of the bar and ordered a Coke. I wasn't alone a minute before I felt someone walk up from behind me and start to rub her hands across my thighs.

"Damn, you a thick nigga. You mind if I sit with you?" Before I could answer, she slipped onto the bar seat across from me while continuing to rub my thighs.

She was a pretty woman, about eighteen, light skinned, slender with perfectly rounded breasts that cried out silicone. She had on enough makeup to ruin her natural good looks and was dressed scantily in a see-through one-piece mesh sundress, accented by six-inch clear plastic pumps. Her hair was done in a pompadour style with enough hair spray to keep it from moving an inch in a hurricane. Her fingernails were painted in a variety of colors, and she had a tattoo across her chest with a baby's bottle on one side and *Passion* on the other. I noticed for the first time that most of the dancers sported the same hairstyle, tattoos, and makeup.

"Baby, why don't you buy Passion a drink," she said.

She smiled as she said it, and I noticed her teeth, or should I say lack of teeth. Every natural tooth in her mouth was replaced with gold. Some of them had letters and symbols carved in them. I could barely make out one word in her golden billboard, *sex*.

"What are you drinking, Passion?"

"Champagne, baby, and if you really want a good show, why don't you get us a private room where we can talk, and I can give you some real special attention."

I knew she was running the typical stripper scam before she started her rap. They promise you a little more than you would usually get, like a lap dance, a slow rub in places they weren't suppose to touch, and promises of heaven for the price of some overly priced champagne and a chance to take every dollar you walked in with.

"Sure, baby why don't you set it all up," I replied, trying to sound helpless and naive.

"You got it, honey. I promise you a night you won't forget, but you're going to have to give up a little money before they let us get personal. The champagne and room cost fifty dollars, and ya know ya still gon' have to pay for me to shake this pretty ass," she continued, turning around and sticking her naked behind in my face and wiggling it sensuously.

I reached into my pocket and peeled off sixty dollars, making sure she got a good view of the wad.

"Get us a real private room, and tip the bartender the extra ten," I said, trying to leer at her as she would have expected and handing her the money. "I've got a lot of money to spend tonight, and I'm going to need some help."

Chapter 12

Passion walked with me hand in hand to the far end of the club where one of the few empty rooms was available. I could see all of the stages as well as the dancers' dressing room so I didn't give her any grief. She left for about five minutes and came back with cheap champagne in a fake-gold ice bucket and two of her friends. Both were dressed scantily in high heels with tattoos on their arms and legs, sporting big hair wigs, one blond and the other bronze. It always struck me as hilarious when I saw black sisters with blond hair. "Hey, baby, I bought a couple of my friends so you don't get lonely or bored as the night goes on," Passion said as Blondie sat on my lap and wrapped her arms around me. Passion and her other friend began opening the champagne and putting out the glasses.

"Passion said you was cute, but I just thought she was lying," Blondie said and laughed at her own statement. Her laugh sounded like a drunken, wounded hyena.

I realized then that all of them were in some degree of intoxication. The only reason Blondie was sitting on my lap was because she was probably too drunk to stand up for any length of time.

Before things could get any further the lights were turned up and the music stopped.

"Gentleman," the deejay announced, "your attention to the main stage, please. I want you to see and enjoy the most beautiful and perfectly built woman on God's green earth. She's sporting a perfect 36-24-36 figure on a five-foot-nine-inch body without the heels and the prettiest eyes and smile you will ever see. If you got a woman at home leave now because you'll never be satisfied with homegirl again. I give you now the lady known everywhere as Perfection." And with that the lights dimmed.

From the middle of the stage a small beam of light appeared. As the very faint music got louder and louder, the light circle got bigger and bigger. In the center of the light stood a woman dressed in a long blue linen trench coat with matching shades, and six-inch light blue lizard pumps. Her hair was slicked back and ran down her back past her shoulders. Her face was absolutely beautiful with full African features and not an ounce of makeup. The blue-green light glowed off her skin. The music was slow and strong and in sync with her dancing, which was deliberate and methodical. Her long, shapely legs tried to escape from the trench coat's confinement. She had runner's legs with thick calves and well-defined but feminine thighs. The six-inch pumps she wore blended into her legs. The trench slowly fell from her body as the men started to surround the stage. Most strippers started their act with some sort of clothes on, usually a bra and panties, and as they danced and received tips they then stripped until naked. Deejays at strip clubs always talk about seven for the top and seven for the bottom. So for the first seven dollars a stripper received she'd take off her bra and after getting the second seven bucks off went the panties. This way the stripper wouldn't waste her time getting naked without receiving any money.

Perfection was different though. She left nothing to your imagination. It was like she understood that no matter how much of her body she showed, men would always want to give her whatever she wanted. When the coat opened and fell to the floor the room became silent, or was it just me who tuned out the rest of the world? She was absolutely beautiful and totally naked. Perfection stood strong and straight, her cinnamon-bronzed skin glowing in the light. Her breasts were uniquely perfect. Different in the sense that they were full and round but where the darker part started, it also was full and round leading to her petite nipples, a nipple on top of a nipple. Her stomach was flat with the first few rows of her muscles well-defined. Her body was covered with oil, and the light hair covering her vagina glistened in the light. Her ass was perfectly round, and I could imagine sitting a wineglass on it and the wine glass never falling. She started the dance with a pirouette as if to show the entire club what perfection looked like. Even the men who were seated with dancers in front of them couldn't help but sneak a look.

I found myself standing in the doorway staring at her and wondering how any woman could be so perfectly built. As I watched her, I began to see a noticeable difference in the way she danced. Like the kid said out front, she showed as little of herself as any black dancer I've ever seen. Most dancers in black clubs will go so far as to spread their legs as wide open as they can and touch their toes when onstage. This sort of teasing made most men line up after the stage dance begging for the dancer to come to their table for a private dance. The only problem with that is a private table dance costs ten dollars each.

I've seen many a brother go home broke and alone after spending the majority of his money on table dances waiting for the dancer to be as "open" as she was on stage. Some of the dancers were more revealing if you can believe that during the private dances.

Perfection's performance was classy and sensuous. She moved and enticed without giving you the rawness that some dancers have to give to entertain and be paid. Perfection was elegant and graceful, womanly and sexy. She danced for three straight songs, and by the time she was finished, the stage was covered with money and her skin and smile were glowing in the light from perspiration. The crowd clapped wildly, and for the first time that night, I sensed an uneasiness in her. She seemed shy and out of place after the music stopped. She continued to pick up the money while trying to keep herself covered without stopping to put the trench coat back on. One of the bouncers met her at the foot of the stage, helped her down, and escorted her to the dressing room.

As I started back to the seat, Blondie and her friend were hugged up next to each other on the couch with a glass of champagne, whispering and giggling at each other, oblivious of everything around them. Passion was another story: if looks could kill, I would probably be dead. She was sitting on the couch with a glass of champagne in one hand and one of her pumps in the other.

"What the fuck y'all see in that bitch," she spitted out angrily. "That ho don't even show shit. She can't dance, and she don't want nothin' to do wit y'all poor-ass niggas, but y'all would eat her shit if she asked y'all to."

"Damn, Passion, why you got ta be a player hater like that," Blondie said laughingly from the couch. "Ya know if ya could git niggas to fall over ya like that you'd be the happiest bitch in the world."

Before Passion could reply, Blondie's friend said, "Passion, if ya could make half the money homegirl making, ya could get all dem rotten-ass gold teeth replaced."

Blondie and her friend both continued to giggle, and you could see Passion starting to change colors.

"Okay, ladies, let's give Passion a break. Why don't you two do me a favor," I said, reaching into my pocket and getting two fifty-dollar bills. "Why don't you each take one of these and give Passion and me a chance to talk?"

"Well, excuse us," Blondie said in a huff as she emptied her glass and grabbed her girlfriend and both of the fifty-dollar bills and stormed out of the room.

"Are you okay, pretty lady? Would you like some more champagne?" I asked, sitting down next to her and filling her glass without waiting for an answer.

"I hate those bitches. I don't know why I asked them to join our party," she said, downing the glass in one quick gulp and reaching for the bottle for another. Before she could fill her glass I took the bottle from her and poured it myself. I wasn't sure she could even do that herself in the drunken, pissed-off state she was in.

"Passion, how much money do you make on a night like this?"

"Baby, I don't know, about five hundred dollars for a full night. I been on my feet all night. Why don't you take me to a nice hotel and let me show you how great I can make you feel?" she replied, slurring every word.

"Baby, I've got a better idea. I want to meet the lady who just finished dancing."

"Nigga, what do you want with that bitch when ya got me here just throwing my shit at ya? You think that bitch is better than I am?"

"You're reading me wrong, baby. This is business, nothing personal. You bring her here for me to meet, and don't tell her a thing. Here's three hundred dollars and I promise you a night out on the town next week. I'll take you to a nice restaurant far away from this club," I said, reaching back into my pocket and getting three one hundred dollar bills.

"Fuck you, nigga, I ain't no lapdog for you or anyone else," she spat out, ignoring the money and slumping even further into the sofa.

"Baby, don't be stupid. You ever hear the saying don't let your money get mad? Don't throw away more money than you make on most days just because you're a little jealous."

She thought about what I was saying for a second and then asked, "You promise to take me out next week, right? Anywhere I want to go?"

"Dinner and dancing anywhere, as long as you promise to let me treat you like a lady and understand this has nothing to do with sex. Deal?"

"Damn, you're strange," she said, slowly getting up and getting herself together. "You gon' give me the whole three hundred dollars if I go bring that bitch out here, right?"

"Here, baby," I replied, handing her the three one hundred dollar bills. "I can trust you, can't I?"

"Damn, you're weird. I'll get her here even if I got to drag that bitch back here by her hair," she said, smiling without pretense for the first time that night.

Chapter 13

Perfection walked in twenty minutes later, and my world began to change. I immediately felt like I was in over my head. I started to lose control internally, and I knew then that I should have called this off and just gone home.

She carried herself as if she owned the world. She was dressed in a white satin teddy with a matching robe. She laid down a towel on the seat next to me and sat down on it, gracefully crossing her long, shapely legs.

Reaching out her hand to shake mine she said, "Hello, my name is Micah, and I heard you have a pocket full of money and want to spend all of it on me. Is this true?"

Her voice had a raspy, deep-throat sound that didn't quite fit her. It reminded me of the way Lena Horne's voice sounded when she wasn't singing.

"Good evening, Micah. I thought your name was Perfection."

"Perfection is my stage name, handsome, but you seem safe, so you can call me by my real name, which is Micah," she said with a smile, looking directly into my eyes.

"To get back to your question, I hadn't planned on spending all of my money on you or anyone else in particular until I saw you on that stage. How did you get so good? You looked so comfortable until it came time for you to pick up your money. Would you like something to drink?" I asked, pointing to the half-empty champagne bottle.

I had no idea where I was going with this conversation but I was feeling confident that just by talking to her, it would take us somewhere.

Her eyes opened wide, and she said, "Thank you, but I don't drink alcohol or smoke. You're probably the only person here to recognize that I am uncomfortable taking money from men who in most cases should be bringing it home to their kids. But I am impressed by your observation, and I'm not that easily impressed."

"Well, that makes two of us. I've seen many a woman strip before, but none with the class and beauty you show. You have no tattoos, you're in excellent shape, you speak with such grace, you don't drink or smoke, and with that said I can't help but ask what the hell are you doing here?"

She looked at me slyly and said, "I'd like to know the same thing about you. I noticed you immediately as did every other woman in the club. You're very handsome, educated, well-spoken, and you are fine. I'd be hard-pressed to believe there aren't at least twenty women knocking at your heart right now."

"Funny you should say that. But, there are only two women in my life. My wife, who was murdered recently, and my nine-month-old daughter, who will have to spend the rest of her life never knowing how much her mother really loved her."

I don't know where that came from. It wasn't the way I had intended to broach the conversation but everything changed as soon as I let the words out of my mouth. I realized then that she knew who I was, and she knew about Andrea. In that brief second, she changed into a totally different person right before my eyes. Her eyes were now as cold as a winter night, and her face immediately became hard with no signs of the vibrancy and control she initially showed.

"I'm sorry to hear that, but I hope you realize you won't find the love you're missing in a place like this," she said, waving her arm around the room.

"I'm not looking for love here. We both know this place is strictly about the Benjamins, just like we both know I came here looking for the woman whose life my wife traded hers for."

She started to rise and said, "I don't quite understand what that has to do with me or anyone else here. I don't understand why you loonies insist on fucking up a working girl's night."

"Don't play dumb, Micah. You live in Hidden Hills, you killed a guy who tried to kill you in your own home, and you know he killed my wife thinking she was you. Don't you feel at least a little guilty? Have you ever thought about what will happen to my daughter, growing up without a mother, and me without a wife? All I want you to tell me is, why? Why did my wife die? Who are you?"

"I don't know what you're talking about, crazy man. I think you'd better leave before I have you thrown out," she said, sounding more and more agitated.

Before I could say anything, the gorilla that helped her off the stage appeared in the doorway.

"Ya got a problem here, Perfection?"

"Yeah, Jimbo. This nigga here is going through the loss of a loved one and has come to the wrong place for condolences.

Get his ass out of here for me, baby," she said, moving closer to him.

"No problem, baby," Jimbo said, stepping toward me, trying to grab me by the arm.

I knocked his hand away from me with a simple gesture, and I saw a lightbulb go off in his head. For the first time in a while I think he knew he was dealing with more than a simple drunk. He put his right hand in his pocket, but when he took it out he had nothing in it. I should have known it was a distraction but I wasn't thinking straight. I didn't see his left fist as he hit me directly on my temple. I saw stars flash across my eyes as well as felt his arms wrapping around my chest and squeezing the breath out of my lungs. I head-butted him in the face, and as he let me go, I tried to kick him where I thought his balls would be. My foot hit something, and I heard him grunt. The next thing I felt was a sharp pain in my midsection, which buckled my knees. I started to rise and got hit again in the kidney. I couldn't see where the blows were coming from but I raised my arms and started to roll away from the direction of the last blow.

Out of nowhere I heard a somewhat familiar voice, "Okay, boys and girls, the party's over. Why don't y'all let Atlanta's Finest take over from here?"

I raised my head from the floor, barely able to keep my dinner down, and standing in the doorway was Detective Harris with his badge out and gun pointing at no one in particular, smiling as if he was watching a circus act.

Chapter 14

"Would you like to tell me what the hell you were doing in there?" Detective Harris asked.

We were sitting in his car a couple of blocks from the club. I had an ice pack pressed against my temple with my head tilted against the back of the seat.

"You know why I was in there. What the hell were you doing there? Are you following me now?" I asked, trying to gain my composure. I've been working so hard to stay in control but I guess I haven't done a good job at that this entire night.

"Contrary to popular belief, I do have other things to do besides watch over you. You still didn't answer my question. Why were you harassing that dancer?"

"Detective Harris, let's stop bullshitting each other. You don't play the dumb role well at all. You know she's the lady who killed that Bradley character. And you know why I'm here. I told you before that I'm going to find out why my wife was killed and who signed her death warrant. Micah's the answer to all my questions."

"Okay, you're not dumb, but did you actually think by approaching her she would automatically embrace you and spill her guts. On one hand she is as ruthless as the person she killed is or on the other hand she could be a manipulative opportunist who put your wife's life at risk for reasons neither you nor I can understand. I want to know why your wife died almost as bad as you do, but the woman's clean. She has no record and no history that I or anyone else in the department can find. I shouldn't be telling you any of this but you've got to back off and let me do my job."

"Don't waste your breath, detective. I'm in this until the end. I owe my wife at least that much. Let me help you! I can go places your badge and your oath to the department won't let you. I also think you'd be surprised at the resources I have at my disposal."

He laughed at me. It's been a long time since anyone laughed at me to my face.

"Before I lose my temper and get arrested for beating you to a pulp, at least explain to me what's so funny," I said.

"You are. I've seen men break down and cry over the death of their wives, I've seen them become uncontrollably violent, verbally and physically, and some men have become walking zombies. You're different. I don't know what kind of love you shared with your wife but I do know it must have been the kind most of us dream of one day having. But, I won't risk twenty years of service by sanctioning an unlicensed neophyte to become involved in a multiple murder case."

"I'm not letting this go, and you'll be seeing me again, detective," I said as I started to reach for the door handle.

Detective Harris grabbed my shoulder, pulling me back into my seat and said, "Hold on a second." He reached into the backseat and picked up a manila folder. "I could lose my job for this but a number of the things we talked about at our last meeting bothered me. I'm going to give you an opportunity to back up all of that posturing you did. There's a guy I put in prison who's going to be released tomorrow morning. His name is Bishop. He has no idea that I pulled a couple of strings and he's getting out early but he's going to need some help getting back on his feet. You need someone who can walk the walk where you've never been, and he needs a reason for not wanting to go back to the life he lost." And with that he handed me the file. "The system screwed him but he thinks I did the screwing. Look at the file, it's his life. If you decide to help him don't mention my name. You need to understand that I could lose my twenty-year pension for this. I'm giving your self-righteous ass an opportunity to help a brother, I think the two of you can go places I can't and do things my badge won't allow me to."

"Why are you doing this now? You don't owe me anything, or do you? I bet there's more to all of this than even you can handle," I declared, picking up the folder from my lap and turning it over and over, in my hands without opening it.

"I ain't telling you any more than I have already. But, I will tell you this much, I ain't never went after anyone because of the color of his skin. I put drug dealers, rapists, and murderers behind bars because that's what I get paid to do, and that's where they belong. I ain't a racist but I do hate people who try to circumvent the system. Bishop made a lot of important people scared and jealous. He got set up. If he was white, it probably wouldn't have happened, but he ain't white. I like his guts. He was born into the system but he beat the system. Go home and read his damn file. Be there tomorrow, and with Bishop's help, you may get all the answers you've been searching for. Before you go, answer a question for me: What kind of music do you listen to?"

"What the hell do you want to know that for?" I asked, bewildered that the conversation was switching so dramatically and wondering what game was this white man playing this time.

"Relax, man, it's just a question."

"I listen to all kinds of music, why?"

"I know this guy who considers himself a rapper. One of those hardcore-kill-the-police-and-destroy-the-government types. He gave me a copy of a demo CD to pass around, and since I'm doing you a favor, I was wondering if you could give it a listen when you get a chance and tell me what you think, I'd appreciate it," he said, handing me a CD.

I took the disc knowing good and well that I wasn't about to sit down and listen to some dumb rap CD, especially for Detective Harris. I put the CD in the file and asked him to drop me off at my car.

I held my curiosity in check until I got home and settled in bed. My stomach continued to feel like it wanted to regurgitate, and my face had started to swell. The headache alone would have kept me up anyway.

The file Detective Harris had given me was composed of old newspaper clippings, police reports, college and high school records, probation interviews, and a couple of pictures of Bishop.

The most recent showed he was a lanky guy; light bronze skin; long shoulder- length hair tied back in a ponytail; prominent chin with thin lips; and a pointed nose. My daddy would call him a white black boy. The thing that struck me the most was his dead eyes. His eyes were a dark brown, but they seemed void of any emotion. Maybe it was just the picture.

The *Reader's Digest* version of one "Bishop Wind" read like a Snoop Doggy Dogg music video. His crackhead mother abandoned Bishop by the time he was three. He spent the next few years being shuffled from one family member to another, never staying more than a year at any place. Sometimes he was asked to leave other times he just left. According to this report the only place he felt comfortable was at his grandmother's. But, by the time he was fifteen, even after spending four years with her, he had decided he was old enough and smart enough to take care of himself. Bishop started selling crack on the street corners and pimping his middle-class strung-out housewives. Within three years Bishop had a thriving operation, and was one of the most feared street hustlers around. Rumor had it that he personally supervised and participated in many of the murders involving rival gangs and snitches while amassing a small fortune. Detective Harris's notes never mentioned what, but something happened to Bishop. The next information dated six months after a botched attempt on his life by a rival gang that left him in the hospital with multiple gunshot wounds. He survived all of that only to disappear for six months before showing up long enough to turn over the reins of his gang to his first lieutenant, Delmar Cole. He then enrolled in a small private college and spent the next three and a half years attending school, working on the side teaching tennis and bartending while maintaining a perfect 4.0 grade point average in business management. He had one more semester left when his life took another 360-degree turn. Delmar was ambushed and killed by Bishop's longtime rival Darth Kevinezz. Darth was found days later with his heart cut out within blocks of Bishop's house. Bishop was promptly arrested and charged with murder, on from what I could see was strictly flimsy evidence.

Bishop had been in jail about six months now, and I was sure he didn't have any chance of getting back in school since most schools now had honor codes. I'd be so pissed if something like that had happened to me, and I definitely wouldn't want to help some stranger on a wild-goose chase after a beautiful stripper and looking for some mystery man.

I didn't have many options now, though. I couldn't show myself in the club anymore. Micah knew what I looked like, and I knew she was not going to talk to me, but she was the key. I had no choice but to get some help.

Why this guy would even consider helping me was the question. I've got money, so I could afford to pay him if I needed to, but how the hell was I supposed to trust a known killer and drug dealer? Better yet, how did I know Detective Harris wasn't setting Bishop and me up for a fall? I had so many questions and nowhere near enough answers.

Chapter 15

When I finally got to sleep, I dreamed about the night Andrea and I created our daughter.

Andrea always enjoyed being wined and dined, and I knew she was going to be late getting home this particular Friday night. I spent the early part of the day shopping at the Lenox Mall in Buckhead. The Lenox Mall is a perfect icon in Atlanta for overindulgence. From the curbside valet parking, fully uniformed concierge, five-star restaurants and hotel, to some of the most expensive stores in Georgia, Lenox has it all. It had been renovated recently and another level had been added with around thirty specialty stores and restaurants. Even though Lenox was created exclusively for the rich and famous, the majority of its day-to-day clientele was middle-class Atlanta natives and teenagers, black and white, from all over Atlanta and its suburbs. They hung out mainly in the lower level where the inexpensive fast-food restaurants held court and the eight-screen movie theater was located.

I spent most of my time in the few women's specialty stores that I knew my wife liked. After picking up a few things, I stopped at the florist and grabbed some peach tulips and a new crystal vase. Most women loved roses but Andrea had an affinity for tulips. I then went to my friendly neighborhood supermarket. I remember when I was a kid you had the little mom-and-pop grocery stores right around the corner. You could always go in and know everyone there, shop for your fresh meat and seafood, and most of the time put it on the bill your folks arranged to pay every other payday. Those days were gone and the big football field-size corporate stores had taken over. The prices were better but I still missed the security I got from the corner stores.

I've always considered myself a good cook. My dad had taught me a lot of New Orleans, style dishes when I was younger, and I've always felt comfortable around a stove. Andrea loved this since she didn't know how to boil water when we first got married. I had taught her how to prepare a number of dishes, and she had gotten better at cooking, adding her own special touches. But tonight, I was going to make her favorite meal. At the grocery store I picked up a number of things: a couple of thick catfish fillets, a head of lettuce, some lemons, a can of mandarin orange slices in a heavy sauce, a couple of baking potatoes, poppy-seed dressing, a packet of Cajun seasoning, onions, green peppers, shallots, frozen peas, and a gallon of pineapple sorbet.

I spent the first couple of hours after getting home cleaning the house. I laid out the white silk teddy with its matching lace full-length robe and slippers I had bought at Lenox. I then went downstairs and started dinner. I washed and laid out the fish in a glass pan with butter, onions, green peppers, and Cajun seasoning. I washed the baking potatoes and sprinkled salt over them while they were still wet, then wrapped them in aluminum foil and placed the potatoes in the oven to bake first, since they took the longest. Andrea never had the patience for the oven; she liked to just dump them in the microwave and hit ten minutes. I always complained that the potatoes tasted dry that way, but she'd just look at me like I was a dummy and continued to microwave them to death.

After the potatoes had been in about thirty minutes, I lowered the temperature and slid the fish in then started on the salad and began setting the table. I pulled out our finest china and accessories and set up the table for two. The atmosphere was completed with candles, the tulips I had purchased earlier, and her favorite mixture of CDs playing softly on the stereo, Sade, Anita Baker, Jodeci, Luther Vandross, and her new favorite, Brian McKnight.

I started the salad by washing the lettuce and tossing it with a little poppy-seed dressing then adding the baby mandarin orange slices, freshly cooked bacon crumbled into small bits, diced boiled eggs, tomatoes, and cucumbers. I sat this in the refrigerator to chill, turned the fillets over, dimmed the lights and proceeded to shower and get myself ready for the night.

I'm not much on robes, or pajamas for that matter, but I met her at the door after hearing her park in the garage wearing the Japanese silk kimono that she had bought for me during one of her many spending sprees. I wrapped my arms around her and kissed her surprised face gently then whispered in her ear that I had been waiting for her and could she humor me by letting me blindfold her. She started to protest but I kissed her again firmly, slowly exploring her mouth with my tongue as I felt her body relax. She dropped her briefcase, turned around and gave in. I covered her eyes with one of her scarves and proceeded to walk her upstairs to our bedroom. She laughed and held on tightly as if she had no idea where she was. I was struck again with her beauty and style as we fumble up the stairs.

We ended up in our bedroom where I slowly undressed her one piece at a time, caressing and kissing each part of her as I uncovered it. By the time I was finished I could feel her heart pounding through her chest and slight tremors attacking her body. I lifted her up as she encircled my shoulders with her arms and laid her head on my chest, I carried her to the garden tub we shared. Somehow I managed to gracefully lay her in the tub still blindfolded and free myself from the kimono. I got in the tub and started to bathe her with her favorite scented soap. I asked her to stand and lean against the stained-glass window that surrounds the tub. As the soap ran down her body, I was again amazed at her physical beauty. Andrea had always worked hard at keeping herself in excellent condition. Running, working out on the StairMaster and bicycle, as well as weight conditioning on the circuit weights at the gym. With all that, she never lost her feminine touch and feel. Her breasts were firm but soft, her stomach flat and inviting, her arms and hands strong and wandering, her legs long and defined in the way that made them delectable in or out of heels. Seeing her naked with soap running down her body aroused me like no other woman ever had.

After I bathed her, we relaxed in the tub, listening to the music and drinking Sprite out of champagne glasses. We lost the blindfold somewhere along the way, but it didn't seem to matter.

We started to kiss lightly, the familiar passion building. I brought her to me, face-to-face, and she allowed me to enter her as she sat on my lap. I started to feel my spirit leaving me and my essence being replaced by her spirit. We moved and felt each other, neither of us wanting this moment to end. I stood and after she wrapped her long, elegant legs around my waist, I stepped out of the tub and walked us entwined and wet to the side of the bed.

I laid Andrea on her back and continued to move in and out of her sweet passion. We stayed that way, changing positions and emotions but never losing contact. I have never been more in love in my entire life, never have I felt more loved than at that moment. We ended the way we began, together, laughing, crying, and trembling. Andrea told me between the touching, talking, laughing, and loving, that she believed we had created our first baby. I didn't take her comment seriously at first, but the more I thought about it, the more I knew she was probably right. Andrea had never been wrong about anything when it came to the two of us, and her being pregnant after tonight could be nothing more than the truth.

We eventually made it downstairs to dinner. Andrea said that even though the fish tasted a little dry, it was one of the best meals I'd ever cooked for her.

We ended the night in bed. I never knew sorbet could taste so good when spread over the right body parts.

Chapter 16

I was at the central lockup by 7:00 A.M. I had no idea what time Bishop would be released, so I figured the earlier, the better.

My luck must be getting better in my old age because as soon as I parked, I spotted Bishop coming out of the station. He looked exactly like his pictures except he was about ten pounds lighter. He was dressed in Hilfiger jeans with a long-sleeve jean shirt, and Timberland boots. His skin tone was a lighter bronze than I expected, as if he was of mixed heritage. His hair was coal black and tied into a ponytail that hung to his shoulders. As he walked down the street, other pedestrians made a conscious effort to stay out of his way. He had that thuggish walk that said he owned it all, full of confidence. The scowl on his face was exactly as advertised in his pictures, intense with those dead eyes. He carried a brown paper sack in one hand and a hardcover book in the other.

I moved across the street to cut him off, and he picked me up almost instantly and turned to face me.

I was about five feet from him when I asked, "Are you Bishop?" while reaching out to shake his hand.

"Who wants to know, nigga?" he replied in a low, raspy voice, never taking his eyes off me and not taking my outstretched hand.

"I know this is kind of strange, my brother, but I heard you were getting out today and was told you may be the person who can help me with a problem I have," I replied, putting my outstretched hand back in my pocket while matching his stare.

"I ain't ya brother," he said as he turned his back on me.

"And I ain't no nigga, Bishop," I replied, starting to feel like this whole situation was a waste of time, but finding myself unable to back down and walk away.

Bishop stopped in his tracks, turned completely around and walked straight toward me and got within an inch of my face.

"I don't know you, my brother," he replied, stretching out brother sarcastically. "You walk up on me knowing more about me than I do about you, asking for help. I've been set up once already and now out of the clear blue I'm taken out of my cell and released. I'm not a happy motherfucker at this moment. So don't fuck with me. You look like a straight citizen, go home before you get hurt," he said and turned around and continued on his way.

"Bishop, can I at least give you a ride home or some money to catch a cab?" I asked, following right behind him.

Bishop slowly stopped and turned around with a smile on his face and asked, "What kind of car do you have?"

"Bishop, don't play me for a fool. You saw me when I drove up, and you know I've got a Jag. I'll let you drive if that makes you more comfortable, but you've got to at least hear my story."

"You offered cab fare before. If I take that I don't have to listen to a damn thing, do I?" he replied.

I reached into my pocket and took out a twenty-dollar bill. I held the twenty and in the other hand I held the car keys. "Make up your mind, Bishop: ride the cab in silence or drive the Jag and listen to my story. Decide."

Bishop walked up, still fronting his scowl and grabbed the car keys, saying, "I hate catching cabs," and walked straight to my car. He hit the alarm on the key chain and started to open the door. Looking over the hood, he said, "I want you to know my ride at home is just as bad as this one, and if my crazy-ass sister would have answered her phone, pager, or cell phone I wouldn't be driving nowhere with you."

I smiled and said, "I'm glad she has other priorities," and got in the passenger side of my car.

Bishop drove as if he were born to be in control. We were on the highway and heading downtown within two minutes. He wasn't a reckless driver, but he did drive fast.

"So, who told you I was getting out today? I didn't even know until they roused my ass up at four o'clock this morning to pack my shit," Bishop said while moving in and out of traffic.

"We have a mutual enemy, who has asked not to be identified, believes you and I can help each other. He told me you would be released sometime today, and I agreed to meet you."

A smirk crossed his face, and he said, "A mutual enemy who knew when I would be released, but doesn't want you to tell me who he is. Now who could that be?"

"You act like you know who it is," I said, feeling like both Bishop and Detective Harris were playing me.

"Sounds like Detective Dick is back to his old tricks," Bishop replied while stretching the word *dick* out as long as possible.

"Who is Detective Dick?" I asked, knowing the answer but needing to have it validated.

"I guess you know him by Detective Harris. His street name has always been Detective Dick. We call him that because he's like a horny old man's dick. When it comes to the so-called street thugs, he's always trying to screw ya."

"I don't know anything about that, but he does seem to think you can help me with my problem."

"I ain't helpin' you wit' shit, but tell me about it anyway, we got some time to waste."

I told him everything, Andrea's murder, Detective Harris, Bradley and how he died, and my meeting with Micah. As I told the story he asked a couple of questions, and I could tell I had his attention.

When I finished, we rode quietly for some time, and I could tell he was mulling over what I had said.

"Do ya mind if I make a quick stop before ya drop me off?" he asked.

"I don't care, Bishop, you're driving. But are you going to help me?" I asked, feeling stupid for telling him my problems and even worse for needing his help. I still couldn't get over the fact that this guy has sold drugs to weak, defenseless black people, maybe even kids, and for all I know he could be even a worse killer than the one who murdered my wife.

"I told you before, I ain't helpin' you wit' nuthin'. I feel ya pain but I don't know you from Adam. I got my own life to git back in order. Them assholes stole a lot of time from me while I was rottin' away in that jail on bogus charges that they knew was bullshit. Ya must have really loved ya wife, but I can't help ya. Can I still make my stop?"

"Make your stop, Bishop," I said dejectedly.

We drove in silence for the next twenty minutes and ended up on Lenox Road near the mall. Bishop pulled into a gated entrance to a nursing home that had been built within the last year. The guard at the gate recognized Bishop immediately and buzzed us in.

"I'm going to visit my granma-ma. You can come in if ya want, or you can sit in your car," Bishop said, getting out of the car.

At this point, I couldn't imagine Bishop having a mother, much less a grandmother but I tagged along nonetheless.

Her room was located on the bottom floor surrounded by a man-made lake that ran through the complex.

His grandmother was sitting outside her room in a rocking chair, which seemed to surround and protect her. She looked like one of the Indian wives complete in tribal attire that I had seen in John Wayne westerns. She wore her hair exactly like her grandson, in a ponytail but hers was completely gray and ran down her back to her waist. Her face was beautiful in its own way, with full wrinkle lines, which encompassed her entire countenance. From a distance I could see the main difference between Bishop and his granma-ma. Granma-ma's eyes were alive and dancing, as if she knew all the answers and the questions.

Bishop caught her eye, and she immediately started to smile and raise her petite body from the rocking chair.

"No, Granma-ma, don't get up," Bishop said, rushing the last few yards to her side.

"Boy, who you talking to? You give no orders here," she said in the soft but powerful voice. "You ain't too old that your granma-ma can't still whup ya ass, and how in the hell am I suppose to hold ya if I don't stand up?"

"Granma-ma, why ya got to talk like that," Bishop asked, his face changing colors. If I didn't know any better I would have thought he was blushing.

"For the same reasons you talk like a street thug when you and I both know ya know better," she replied while wrapping her little arms around her grandson's neck.

Bishop looked like a little kid in his grandmother's embrace, not the drug lord we both knew he was.

"When did ya git out, and is this ya probation officer?" she asked, pushing Bishop away and looking in my direction.

Before Bishop could answer I moved to hold her hand and told her, "No, ma'am, my name is Noah Houston, and I'm just an old friend of Bishop's on the way to drop him off at home."

"Now, boy, I liked you until you started lying ta me. Bishop ain't never had no friends like you. Ya older, seem well off, speak real politely, and you ain't carrying no gun. So tell Granma-ma the truth before I have to sic one of my Blackfoot demons on you," she said with a knowing smile.

Bishop looked at me, smiling genuinely for the first time and said, "Don't pay Granma-ma and her demons no mind. She's one-percent pure Blackfoot Indian and she still considers herself a Shaman, even though she has no tribe members to give medicine to."

"Boy, don't speak about me as if I'm not sitting here ready to whup ya butt. I still have my family's ghosts to watch over, young man," she said, addressing me and ignoring Bishop. "We were a proud and strong people, and my grandson is still part Blackfoot so I got to watch over him, too."

"Granma-ma, I just wanted to let you know I was home, and I'll be coming to see you later this week. Are they treating you well?"

"Yes, my little one, and your sister still visit's me a couple of times a week, bringing gifts and junk. I still ain't going to let her buy me anything with that blood money you give her."

"Granma-ma, you know I ain't in that business no more, and the first thing I'm going to do now that I'm out is to get reinstated at school."

"You do that, boy. I prayed hard to the gods for you to leave that life, and I want you back in school. You help him wit' that, Mr. Houston, you hear me," she said, looking me directly in the eyes. Her whole demeanor seemed to change. Her eyes became as cold as her grandson's.

"Yes, ma'am. I don't know what I can do but I'll do what I can."

"Don't worry about that, Granma-ma. I got it all under control. Now I know your birthday is Saturday, so you make sure you put on your pretty blue dress, and I will pick you up at eight as usual," Bishop said, delicately trying to change the subject.

"Boy, ya sure ya got money for that, I don't need to be celebrating another year getting older anyway," she answered, the smile back in her eyes as she looked at him.

"Granma-ma, please don't do this. Be ready at eight. I got to go," Bishop replied, leaning over to kiss her gently on the cheek.

"Good-bye, ma'am. It was nice to meet you, and I hope you have a happy birthday," I said, following Bishop down the walkway as she smiled and waved us away.

Chapter 17

"I hope you didn't get the wrong impression back there," Bishop said after we had been on the road driving in silence for about five minutes. We were heading into the heart of the Atlanta downtown area, with Bishop still at the wheel.

"Is there an impression I should have gotten?" I asked, feeling uncomfortable and wanting this ride to end as soon as possible.

"You just need to know I ain't soft. I love my grandmother, but I'd as soon kill a fucker for stepping in my space as I would squash a nagging fly." As he said the words I could see his eyes become darker and his entire physical disposition change and become harder, more walls erected to protect himself.

"Has this attitude and the hardness you seem to be able to turn on and off at your whim helped to contribute to you being such a big-time drug dealer and pimp?" I asked.

Bishop turned his stare on me for a second, then turned back to the road and said, "I ain't no drug dealer or no pimp. I'm a survivor. Society plotted my course. White folks with all their shit is the society I'm talking about. I was just going along for the ride. He made the drugs available, he created my users, he allowed me to wash my dirty money in his banks where he took his chunk and organized the next shipment. I ain't taking the blame for this country's caste system or for the weak people who would sell their mother for a hit on my pipe."

"But they're your people, your kids out here selling that crap and getting hooked on it at the same time," I said.

"Man, you been watching too much TV. I ain't never had no kids selling my shit. Half these little bastards can't even count to ten. They too busy rapping about a life they don't know nuthin' about. And the kids that are selling ain't got no other choice. They ain't the Cosby kids. Dad ain't never been there, Moms' either working two jobs to stay afloat or strung out on some heavy shit herself. If the government wants to act like they don't exist and can't save these people, who the hell gon' help them but themselves? You think any animal out here is going to starve to death on purpose and not do anything to make a dollar?"

"People act like these kids want to belong to a gang; they want to rob, steal, and kill. They ain't nuthin' but a product of their environment. Seventy-five percent of my mules and clients were white male middle-class corporate fuckers or their wives, anyway. Driving up in their middle-class station wagons with the child seat in the back, wanting to buy weed, crack, and anything else I had to sell. Kind of shocking, ain't it. See they don't show that half of it on the evening news," Bishop continued.

"So you think that makes what you do okay? You didn't use kids to run your drugs, and you sell mostly to white people, and you can't change society ills, big deal. Black man like me glad to know there are real class-conscious black businesspeople out here, like you."

"I'm gon' let that statement walk since I know you ain't thinkin' straight right now wit' ya wife dead, and you don't know why, but don't fuck wit' me, nigga. I don't care how educated you is or how special you is, you bleed just like me, and I done hurt many a man for less than your attitude."

"I'm not worried about you, Bishop. In a street fight, you may be the best there is, but you left that life. You weren't driven out, you left. You started a whole new life, and you were successful. You saw something then about your life, and you decided you didn't like it, and you changed. I've got friends with PhD's who couldn't do what you did. You respect your elders, and no matter what you say, you do care, maybe not about the same things I care about, but you do care."

"How the hell you figure I care about anything? You don't know me. But let me tell ya, I do care about one thing, and that's the almighty dollar bill, the Benjamins, cash money. You been brought up with that platinum spoon in your mouth, and you think you can hang out here with the hard legs. You don't stand a chance. What you gon' do now that I won't help you, go hanging out in nightclubs trying to get some female Rambo to answer your questions, or some white cracker wit' a badge to help lead you in the right direction?" he asked belligerently.

"To be honest, I don't exactly know what I'm going to do, but I won't beg you to be involved. I understand you've got more pressing needs. I will tell you this much though," I said, reaching into the backseat and getting the folder that had been given to me by Detective Harris. "Detective Harris has his own reasons for helping you and me, and I don't think you know any better than me what those real reasons are. You don't even know why he gave me a copy of your entire file," I said, pointing the file at him as I talked.

I had totally forgotten about the CD until it slipped out and fell on my lap. Before I could put it back, Bishop asked, "What's the CD for?"

"Detective Harris asked me to critique the songs on it some local rapper is trying to put out," I answered, finding it hard to accept that Bishop loved changing the direction of any conversation at his whim, but amazed at how his eyes lit up when I mentioned the contents of the CD.

"You mind if I listen to it for the rest of the drive? I'm almost home," he said, grabbing the CD and slipping it into the stereo before I could answer.

"Yeah, why not," I answered sarcastically.

The music started off with a poem by the rapper, talking about the ills of big-city life and the black people's struggle today, 1998. The music in the background was slow and methodical. He spoke of some of the same things Bishop and I was just speaking on: crime, poverty, babies making babies, our modern-day slavery to drugs, the lack of family values and the breakdown of the black man from his woman. From the poem he went into a rap soliloquy about his life and dreams with a strong bass line running softly behind. I had not heard anyone rap like this before, but then again I wasn't a rap connoisseur.

Bishop reached over and turned off the music.

"I don't feel like listening to that boring crap. Do you know who you were listening to?" he asked.

"I listen to rap every now and then but I'm not that familiar with most artists. I would buy this guy's stuff though. Do you know who he is?"

"Naw, I ain't never heard of him but it don't matter. Half of Atlanta's youth, black and white, want to be rappers, and they don't know nuthin' about the industry.

"Do you know anything about the music business?" I asked curiously. For a minute there, as much as he tried to hide it, Bishop seemed extremely interested in the music and the rapper.

"I don't know anything about anything except surviving. I was doing a damn good job of it until someone got jealous," Bishop replied bitterly.

"Do you want me to help you get reinstated to Morehouse? I have a number of connections there that maybe able to help you," I offered, feeling sorry for his grandmother, not for him.

"I don't need your help, I ain't too sure I'm going back to school anyway," he replied but I could tell his attention wasn't in this car.

"So, I guess you just lied to your grandmother," I said, not trying to disguise the disgust in my voice.

"Fuck you, nigga. You don't know what I did. It don't matter anyway, I'm home," he said, pulling into the driveway of one of Atlanta's premier downtown high-rises. The older white doorman had approached the driver's side and waited patiently for a sign Bishop was finished talking. I had been so involved in the conversation I didn't realize how far we had driven or to where. "Take ya psychobabble and lay it on someone else. I would wish you luck but I think you're in way over your middle-class citizen head."

As he turned to open the door, the doorman opened the driver's side and greeted Bishop enthusiastically, "Good morning, Mr. Wind. It's so good to see you again."

"Yeah, Jake, take me up, will you, I don't have my keys," Bishop demanded and slammed the door.

I sat in the car, feeling dead and beaten. I decided then that I couldn't do this anymore. I got out and got in the driver's seat and went to get my daughter. Through all the pain, I realized it was time to let it go. I hoped Andrea could forgive me. I didn't think I would ever forgive myself.

Chapter 18

I picked up Ashley on the way home. I knew my dad wasn't happy about me taking her back to the house but he was glad that I was finished with this so-called wild-goose chase as he described it and getting my life back together. The first thing Ashley and I did was to go straight to our local church and say a prayer for Andrea and to say good-bye. This was the only time since her death that I actually felt like this was a permanent good-bye. Ashley seemed to know exactly what I was doing. She was peaceful during the whole process.

The next couple of months were mere blurs as I tried to keep myself as busy as possible. I spent my early mornings fighting off sleep, after getting just a couple of hours. Ashley was still at the stage where she was getting up once or twice a night looking for a bottle and someone to hold her close. I didn't know if this was from her missing her mother or just being a baby. I still, usually awoke while it was dark out to shower, shave, dress, and start breakfast. After packing Ashley's day bag with the necessary diapers, milk, baby food, and toys, I would then wake her up and dress her for day care. Gina spent the night sometimes when she decided she wanted to mother both Ashley and me. I enjoyed the company and the house didn't seem so lonely when she was around.

Work became my refuge. I realized for me to survive this I would have to submerge myself in anything that would leave my mind very little time for itself.

Stephanie relinquished the reins as soon as I walked in the door. She had done such a great job during my absence that I gave her a round-trip ticket to the Virgin Islands and paid for an all-inclusive suite at one of its nicest villas. She came back tanned, happy, and ready to get back to work.

Even though Bishop had refused to help me, I didn't forget the promise I made his grandmother. I called a few of my friends who were high-ranking alumni at Morehouse and persuaded them to put their two cents in to try and get Bishop reinstated. I also sent his granma-ma a dozen roses and a Blackfoot tribal medicine-man robe I had ordered from a Web site of one of the original Blackfoot reservations in Canada's. With this final act, I washed my hands of Bishop and his problems or so I thought.

My day started off as any typical Friday would except for the fact that Ashley had spent the entire night awake and crying more than usual. She seemed to be teething, and I could barely make out the front two teeth cutting her gums. The Anbesol medicine didn't seem to help at all, so I spent most of the night rocking her in my lap and rubbing the frozen plastic gum soother I had picked up from the drugstore against her poor gums. I couldn't tell you when we finally fell asleep but I awoke the next morning with Ashley cuddled next to me sleeping peacefully. I got up and arranged some pillows around her so she wouldn't fall off my bed, before heading to the bathroom to wash up and get dressed for work.

Before I could make it to the bathroom, the phone rang.

"Good morning, big brother and daddy wanna-be," my always-jovial sister, Gina, said.

"Don't start with me this morning, Skinny. I've been up all night with my crying little princess. These new teeth are killing her, and she hasn't slept much at all the last couple of days," I replied, heading to the bathroom.

"How about you, have you had any sleep lately?" Gina asked, sounding more concerned than I cared to believe. Gina had a way with the dramatics that always left you wondering if she really did care about your situation or if she was just performing for the moment at hand.

"Well, you should know that when she's up, I'm up. All she's got is her daddy."

"Make a deal with you, then, seeing how you haven't had a decent night's sleep lately, and you're probably desperate. Pay my rent for this month, and I'll watch Ashley for the entire weekend. This way my poor big brother can get some rest, and my favorite niece can get a break from your ugly face," she said with a smile I could feel over the phone.

"First of all, what makes you think I don't enjoy sitting up all night playing the perfect daddy?" I replied, having a hard time keeping a smile off my face. My sister has always been the family con, and I was her perfect setup. "And since when did it cost me so much to get you to baby-sit when I know I can get these services from you for free?"

"Look Noah, I need a short-term loan, and you need a break. What's a couple of dollars between family anyway? Don't make me call Daddy and start crying, you know he can't stand to hear me cry."

GJT Simpson

"Whatever, ya big sissy. I'll lend you the money, and I expect to get it back next payday, okay?"

"Sure you will, my handsome brother. What time are you going to drop Miss Ashley off?"

"I'm not. You can meet me at the office this morning and start earning your money," I answered.

"Damn, you drive a hard bargain. That check should be signed and ready when I get there, and it better not bounce," she replied, hanging up the phone after getting what she wanted, as usual. Sometimes being taken by my sister wasn't so bad.

The rest of the day was uneventful, and I found myself in bed and fast asleep by 10:00 P.M.

I was awakened at 3:00 A.M. by the telephone. I figured it was Gina calling to complain about still being awake with my crying princess. Imagine my surprise when I realized it was Bishop on the other end.

"Yo, dawg, this Bishop. Some wanna-be gangsters got ya female Rambo all tied up, and I don't think she's going to live through the night."

Chapter 19

I was in my car and on the road less than five minutes after getting off the phone with Bishop. The only information Bishop would give me was where he was going to meet me, and then he hung up. The directions were to a gas station near Cabbagetown. Cabbagetown is in the heart of Atlanta and is populated predominately by what my daddy would call "po' white trash." Most of the houses and many of the buildings in this area were dilapidated and abandoned. Some were still occupied but most were used by homeless people and drug addicts.

On the drive to meet Bishop, I started to go over the many questions that were running rampant in my head: Who was holding Micah? Why was Bishop trying to help me? Why would anyone want to hurt Micah, and what did it have to do with Andrea's death? I also wondered if I really wanted to get back on this roller coaster. I had spent the last few months building a foundation and coming to grips with the reality that Andrea was dead, and she wasn't coming back. But it hit me as I pulled up to the gas station that I still had a nasty taste in my mouth. A taste that wouldn't go away until I had exacted some vengeance of my own.

Bishop was standing next to his car smoking a cigar when I drove up. He was dressed in black jeans, boots, linen T-shirt, and a lightweight summer topcoat. He looked exactly as he did when we first met, including the dead eyes. He was driving a black 850 BMW with the windows blacked out. I pulled up next to him and rolled down my window.

"Are we going in my car?" I asked, trying to sound and feel brave even though I had no idea what I was getting myself involved in.

"Naw, dawg. Park yours over there in the manager's space. My nigga inside will watch it like it's mine," he said, pointing to a space near the back door.

I parked my car where he told me to and got out.

Bishop took a long pull on his cigar and tossed it away then retreated to his car as I followed. Opening the passenger door, I was greeted by a low growling sound coming from the backseat. It was too dark for me to make out the breed but the hair standing on the back of my neck confirmed it was a dog, and a big one at that.

"Pay no attention to Big Nasty. He's a pussycat until I tell him otherwise," Bishop said with a smirk.

I got in the car still looking over my shoulder at the huge shape in the backseat. As my eyes adjusted to the darkness, I was able to see Big Nasty. He had blue-green eyes that seemed to glow in the dark and a permanent snarl on his face. He looked like a mix between a wolf and a German shepherd. His coat was charcoal black, and he looked like he could be six feet tall if he stood on his hind legs. I couldn't tune out his persistent low growl or the feeling one gets when someone is staring.

"I hope your lady friend is still alive by the time we get back there. These brothers didn't seem to be the patient kind," Bishop said while driving onto the main road then turning right onto one of the side streets.

"Why don't you start at the beginning, Bishop? I haven't heard from you in months, and I've tried to forget about Micah, period. You call up out of the blue like we're old buddies and request my presence because you think Micah's in trouble. I'm stupid enough to be here but tell me exactly what's the situation," I said.

"True that, my nigga. You had to trust me a lot to come here like this but this still your story. I got involved wit' ya girl about a week after you dropped me off. I started hanging around the club getting to know the lay of the land and the key players. Ya girl didn't fit the mold, and the more I checked into her, the more I realized somethin' funny was going on. I done seen many a player in my time but that bitch a true warrior. She walked the club like she owned it. She didn't do any side jobs like the rest of the whores, and I had my boys stress her wit' some serious loot. She always stayed professional like she really didn't need the money and she was doing the job for another reason. She also one of the only bitches in there that didn't have a pimp stealing her action."

"I was watchin' her tonight when one of the bouncers whispered somethin' in her ear and walked her to the back office," Bishop continued, weaving in and out of the side streets, taking us deeper into the city. I waited about thirty minutes before I asked one of the other girls to go git her because I wanted to see her dance. She came back about five minutes later and told me Micah had left thirty minutes earlier. I knew she was lying or was there. Her car was there, and one of my boys said he never saw her leave."

"I hung around for about ten minutes before she was escorted out of the club by two goons both holding her by her arms as if she was drunk and couldn't walk on her own. She had on a pair of dark shades, and I couldn't get a good look at her. They actually dragged her to her car, put her in the backseat, and they drove off. I laid back and followed them here," he said, pointing to a row of condemned two-and-three-story office buildings lining the block. The street was pitch black, and I realized that Bishop had killed the headlights on the car. He slowed down at the first corner where he turned and parked closely to the curb.

"They're up there," he said, pointing across the street at a three-story building on the opposite corner. "I followed them up to the third floor before calling you. You ready to go up and find out what this bitch got to do with your wife being killed?"

Chapter 20

Up until this time, I had rode along listening to Bishop talk and wondering what the hell I'd gotten myself into. I couldn't help but believe that the answers to all of my questions were in that building, but I also didn't know if I had the guts to ask the questions. I knew I was out of my league and should probably call the police but I needed some answers, and the cops weren't going to get me the response I was looking for.

Bishop interrupted my doubts by asking, "Have you ever used one of these before?" as he handed me a nine-millimeter Glock butt first.

I took the gun out of his hands, careful to keep the barrel pointed away from both of us, released the clip, and ejected the live round from the chamber before putting the clip back in. This particular model didn't come with a safety. Most Glocks don't.

"I don't own a gun because I don't believe in them. But I've had a little experience and even I know you should never travel with a round chambered in a gun that doesn't even have a safety," I said, tossing him the bullet and tucking the gun in my waistband.

Bishop laughed low in his throat and said, "You full of surprises, ain't ya, dawg. You rollin' with this like ya born in drama. I figured the moment you saw that gun you'd freeze and want to go home."

"I'm not the only one full of surprises. You still haven't told me why you're putting your neck out for some fool chasing a dream," I replied, reminding him of the last words he spoke to me when I dropped him off at his apartment.

"We don't have time to get into dat. Here's the plan. I cased the joint, and we can get in from the back door. Once in, we'll take the stairs to the third floor. They are in an open area, so we gon' have a hard time sneakin' up on 'dem, but we got surprise and Big Nasty on our side. Don't be afraid to use that piece, dawg. I ain't got time to baby-sit yo ass. Dem some bad niggas up there, and they'd kill ya much less look at ya." And with that he got out of the car with Big Nasty close on his heels.

I followed them to the back of the building where the door was propped open with a beer can. The inside was dark but Bishop followed Big Nasty who seemed to know just where he was going.

Bishop whistled softly when we got to the stairs, and Big Nasty stopped in his tracks and looked back at him. Bishop turned around and showed me his gun. I took mine out of my waistband, and Bishop whistled again and Big Nasty started up the stairs with us close behind, Bishop on the right wall and me on the left.

At the top of the third floor, the light was intense. The windows had been covered up so there was no way I could have known there was someone up there. The room was large and sparse. In the center was a long table with four chairs arranged haphazardly around it. At the head of the table sat Micah. She was naked and tied with rope to the chair. I had only seen Micah once before but seeing her like this made my heart cry out for her. I was amazed at the hatred that sparked from her eyes, but there was no fear. She kept her eyes on her captors, and if looks could kill, they would both be dead. Strapped helplessly in that chair she still gave off an aura of danger.

One of the guys was sitting in a chair across from Micah, slowly dragging on a fat cigar. I figured he was about six feet six inches and a hefty three hundred pounds while his partner who was on the other side of the table playing solitaire, was the exact opposite in build, a scrawny, skinny man whose feet barely touched the ground as he sat. He couldn't have been more than five feet tall and about one hundred and fifty pounds.

Before we could go any farther the big guy said to Micah, "Bitch, I'm going to ask you this shit one mo' time. Who the fuck are ya and why the hell ya been following my boss?"

Before Micah could so much as open her mouth, he took the cigar from his mouth and placed the burning end roughly against her naked thigh, twisting it as he pressed. Micah flinched but didn't say a word. Tears started to flow from her eyes but she didn't stop looking at him.

The big man removed the cigar and started to laugh, saying to his partner, "This ho is bad, Leroy. I know some niggas who'd be shittin' all over themselves by now."

"Why the hell you didn't give the ho a chance to answer, Gumbo? I wonder about yo ass sometime. You into pain too fucking much. Let's just get our info, kill the bitch, and get back to the club. You know I got to bring that bitch Passion home if

I'ma gon' get some pussy tonight," Leroy replied.

Before Gumbo could respond, Bishop tapped me on the shoulder and pointed to Leroy. He then stood and hollered "kill" to Big Nasty, pointing at Gumbo, while walking confidently toward the bigger man who Big Nasty was flying toward at that point.

Everything moved in slow motion for me. I found myself moving swiftly across the room, pointing the gun at Leroy and screaming for him to raise his hands and kneel down. Out of the corner of my eye I could see Bishop's dog hitting Gumbo right in the chest while growling and trying to tear at his neck. The big guy retreated, screaming and trying to protect his face and neck, with his hands and arms. Bishop was walking slowly toward him with a smile spread from ear to ear and his gun pointed at the man. Leroy got my attention as I watched him jump up and start to run toward a door I hadn't seen when I first looked at the room. I didn't want to shoot him in the back, so I ran after him, closing the gap in no time and kicking him square in the crack of his ass, sending him flying through the air and hitting the wall. I stuck the gun that felt so foreign in my hands into my belt and grabbed him by the collar. I angrily threw him against the wall with every bit of strength I could muster. I stopped for a second wondering where this desire in me to hurt him was coming from. Leroy lay silently on the floor like a sack of potatoes, twitching in his lower extremities. I turned around and saw the big guy crawled up in a corner, holding his throat, blood running down his arms and Big Nasty just sitting and watching, waiting for him to move. Bishop was untying Micah, who seemed to be taking all this in as if it happened every day.

I checked Leroy for weapons and found a small caliber pistol in an ankle holster strapped to his leg. I grabbed him by his collar and dragged him to the table, then threw him roughly into one of the still-standing chairs.

Micah rose from her chair, trying to show none of the signs of a person who had just been kidnapped and physically abused. With tears still streaming down her face she looked at me and asked softly, "What the hell are you two doing here?"

Chapter 21

"Let's go man, this bitch is crazy. We just saved this ho from gettin' her ass killed, and she wants to know what the hell we're doin' here," Bishop said incredulously.

"Call me a bitch or a whore again, and I'll fuck your dumb ass up permanently," Micah replied, looking Bishop straight in the eyes and moving in his direction.

I moved between them, noting how beautiful Micah's body looked naked and glistening with sweat and began to feel guilty about my thoughts.

"Both of you calm down. This is more than any of us gambled on. Put on some clothes, Micah, and Bishop, give me your phone so I can call the police," I said, trying to put some order to this confusion.

"Before we do any of that, I want you to answer my

question. What are you two doing here?" Micah asked again while trying to put on a one-piece summer dress that was draped across a chair.

I could see that she was trembling from the effort, but I didn't know if she would let me help her so I just stood there and looked.

"Micah, you know who I am, and you know who helped that fool kill my wife. I want that person dead or behind bars. Bishop followed you here, calling himself trying to help me. Why, I don't know, and I really don't care if it helps me find the person behind my wife's murder," I said.

"And your pretty black ass would be dead now if we hadn't stuck our noses in your business, you ungrateful bi... " Bishop began.

"Watch your mouth, fool. I don't make idle threats," Micah said, cutting Bishop off mid-sentence, staring him down with the same look of death I recognized in him the first time we met.

Bishop started to finish his statement but decided against it and just smiled in her direction while taking a seat in one of the empty chairs. He called Big Nasty to his side, and the dog reluctantly obeyed.

Micah walked over to me and before I could stop her, she took the gun out of my belt.

"Before you call the police, I have a few questions I need to ask these assholes," Micah said, walking toward Gumbo, who was still sitting on the floor against the wall bleeding from Big Nasty's attack. I started to stop her but Bishop raised his hand and motioned me to hold up.

Micah leaned close to the big guy's face and whispered something in his ear. I couldn't hear what she was saying but I could see the fear amplified in his face. He started to say something to her, and before he could finish the word *bitch*, she stepped back and shot him in his forehead.

I had never seen someone shot in real life before, and it was nothing like on TV. He ended up with a small hole in the middle of his head, but the wall was splattered with gray matter and blood accompanied by a smell that was totally nauseous and indescribable. I felt weak in the knees, and my mouth made motions but no words came out. Bishop was smiling like he was watching a funny movie.

"Damn, Rambo, why ya had to shoot fat boy! It looked like he was about to pay you a compliment," Bishop said while lighting a new cigar.

Micah looked at him as she walked toward Leroy and said, "Didn't your mother ever tell you smoking causes cancer?"

"Naw, she neva told me anything like that but she did tell me to stay away from crazy Rambo wanna-bes," Bishop replied, smiling at their banter.

Leroy was still sitting halfway unconscious where I had thrown him, but he seemed to wake up once he realized Micah was headed in his direction.

"Don't shoot me, lady, I ain't done you nothin'. I just was followin' instructions. Please don't kill my ass."

"What's wrong, midget man? Everybody has to die sometime, and you sure weren't too concerned with killing me so you could go get you some 'stuff' earlier, were you?" Micah replied, closing the distance and jacking a round into the chamber.

"Come on, lady. I don't want to die. Look, I can even tell you about your sister!" he hollered at her while trying to raise his hands to cover his face as Micah put the gun to his forehead.

Whatever that meant, it worked. Micah stepped away from him, and I could see pain etched across her face.

Stepping closer to him, Micah grabbed him by his hair roughly and said, "Motherfucker, don't lie to me. Your life depends on how you answer this: Do you know where I can find my sister?"

Chapter 22

"Boss, you gon' let her talk to me like that? I thought she didn't believe in cursing. She come in here and kill one perfectly good nigga before we can get any info, now she cursing short stuff and 'bout to blow his brains out. Can't get nothing resolved she keep killin' everybody," Bishop proclaimed still sitting in his chair with his cigar burning brightly.

Things were moving fast, and I was still trying to get my mouth to catch up with my brain. I didn't know if Bishop was joking or if he was really looking for me to stop Micah. I knew he was right, and that we needed to keep this guy alive but Micah seemed hell-bent on getting her answers. Standing there with one dead guy in the corner, Bishop rubbing his dog's head and smoking that stupid cigar, and Micah one step away from killing someone else, I realized that I was making some progress.

"Bishop, you know as well as I do that I've got about as much control over Micah as you do. If she's going to kill Leroy here, that's between her and her God," I answered, taking a seat behind Micah and her gun, making it clear to Leroy that I wanted to be out of the way of any stray bullets.

"Come on, man, you can't just let her kill me. What about my rights?" Leroy cried, trying to get from under Micah's grip.

"Nigga, fuck your rights. You better start talking or you're going to be dead like your friend. That fucker shouldn't have burned me with his fucking cigar, anyway. Shit, I might as well just kill your ass, too. I'm going to find my sister anyway, probably don't need your help," Micah said, putting the barrel in the middle of Leroy's chest.

"Okay, okay," Leroy replied, resolved to save his life no matter who he had to give up. "Your sista ran off wit' that rapper fool. We been trying to find him and her for the longest. When you showed up at the club asking all those damn questions, Dominique figured you knew where they were and was coming in for the rescue. We didn't even know she was ya sister until Dominique got word from one of his hush-hush friends. That's why he sent my nigga after you the first time. If I would have been with him, we wouldn't be dealing with this here drama and yo ass would be dead," Leroy continued.

Before he could say another word, Micah flipped the gun in her hand so that she was holding it by the barrel and hit Leroy square in the face with it, sending teeth and blood flying across the floor along with Leroy's semi-limp body.

"He sure wasn't holding shit back, black. Why ya had to hit the nigga so hard? The story was just getting interesting," Bishop said, rising from his chair and grabbing Leroy by the collar with one hand and throwing him casually back into the chair.

"Damn, woman, why ya had to hit my ass," Leroy mumbled through the broken teeth and blood. "I was just stating the obvious. Wasn't nothing personal, strictly business."

"Who is this rapper Darquita left with, and why did she have to leave anyway?" Micah asked, moving closer to Leroy and switching the gun into its proper shooting position.

"So is this what all this shit is about for you, Ms. Rambo? I guess Darquita is ya sista's name, uh? Does she look as good as you do naked?" Bishop asked Micah, smiling mischievously as he sat down, cigar in hand.

Micah was still beautiful in her sundress but the burn on her leg looked bad.

Micah gave Bishop her I'll-kick-your-ass look and kept on directing questions at Leroy.

"Answer my question, dumbass, or do I have to hit you again?"

"Okay, okay. That chump Prophet. They both disappeared after he signed on with my boss's music company. Boss had major plans for his ass, and he just up and disappears."

"When you say Boss are you talking about Dominique?" I asked, trying my best to keep up with all the players.

"Who the hell else ya think I'm talking about. You chumps don't know what the fuck y'all den got y'all self involved with. We talking big money here, and Dom don't like losing any kind of property or money. That fool Prophet was both his money and his property."

"Nigga, please. Dominique ain't smart enough to own shit. He ain't nothing but a front for some white boys who don't want their people to know they sweating niggas and selling drugs and pussy," Bishop kicked in.

"Yeah nigga, I don heard that rumor for as long as I been working for Dom. But he the only nigga touching green as far as I know. If there is someone else above him, I don't want to know.

Dominique scary enough," Leroy continued

"So how bad you think Dominique is gon' hurt you after he finds out you gave us all this information?" Bishop asked.

Before Leroy could answer, Micah jumped in, "Dominique ain't going to find out Leroy told us anything."

"Damn, girl, the only way he ain't gon' find out is for you to kill him. You ready to wax his ass in cold blood?" Bishop asked, looking more happy than concerned.

"Just let me use your phone, Bishop," Micah responded, ignoring Bishop's question altogether.

"Sure, baby, just don't make any long-distance calls," Bishop replied, handing Micah his phone and laughing at his own joke.

"Before you call anyone, Micah, let me look at that burn, and why don't you put your coat back on," I said moving toward her with the coat.

Micah slid her arms into the lightweight trench coat and looked surprised at my concern. She turned around, and I tied the belt around her waist.

"Don't worry about the burn, I'll take care of it later," Micah said as she started to dial a number I couldn't see.

"This is Micah," she said into the phone when someone answered. "I need a cleanup. One dead and one alive. I need the breathing one locked down until I say let him go." She asked Bishop for the address and told the person on the phone the location.

"I also need a safe house outside of Atlanta. Preferably isolated and farther north with food for three for about a week. I'll also need the usual clothing and equipment left for me, hardware and software included."

She held on for a couple of minutes then hung up. "Can

and regroup and figure out our next move. That way we can both get all of our questions answered once and for all."

"Hold on, woman, what about me? I've got a good deal of my time invested in both your life and Noah's, and I'm not inclined to let either of you just abandon me on the side of the road like my usefulness is now over," Bishop announced.

"What happened to the street talk, Bishop? For a moment there you sounded as educated as you really are," Micah asked, staring him down.

"You and Micah both need to slow down, Bishop," I said, standing between them and directing my next comment to Micah. "I've got one question for you before I agree to do anything with you or for you, lady. Who the hell are you, really?"

"Stupid question, Noah," she replied, turning her back to me. "I'm Micah, and I'm looking for my missing sister. This asshole and his friends," she said, pointing to Leroy who was still slumped half conscious in the chair with his head on the table, "drove her off, and I plan on finding her and bringing her back home. Anything else you need to know?" she asked, turning back around and facing me after putting some distance between the two of us.

"I'm going to ask this question one more time. Who the hell are you, really? No one I know can do the things you've demonstrated over just the last hour the way you fight, the viciousness you display, your ability to handle pain, and let's not talk about the cryptic phone call you just made. Now save the next stupid answer you were going to give me and tell me the truth or I'm out of here."

"Like I told you before, I'm just a dancer looking for my

sister," Micah replied.

"Let's go, Bishop. Micah can definitely handle this herself," I said, turning my back to them both and heading toward the stairs and out of this hellhole.

Micah ran to my side, brushing her breasts against me. Holding me by my arms and looking directly into my eyes, she whispered, "Please trust me. I will tell you and Bishop everything, but not here, not now. Come with me to the cabin, and I give you my word I will clear everything up and answer all of your questions."

Chapter 23

The next few hours were a blur, but during that time I learned just how connected Micah is. She borrowed Bishop's phone again and made a number of calls. I couldn't make out what she was saying during most of the conversations but after she finished the last call she announced we would be leaving for Helen in the next twenty minutes. Before I could ask what we were going to do with Gumbo's dead body and Leroy she asked Bishop to tie Leroy to a chair and give her his keys. Bishop being Bishop started to put up a fuss but Micah gave him one of her looks, and he threw the keys at her. With keys in hand she told Bishop to meet us downstairs after he was finished and grabbed me by the hand and led me downstairs to the street.

"I'll assume the BMW is Bishop's. Let's get in and wait for Mr. Wonderful," Micah said sarcastically, opening the driver's side door and getting behind the wheel. I got in on the passenger side, feeling tired and drained.

"I need to ask you something, and I need the truth from you," Micah said, looking me directly in the eyes. "Do you really think you can trust Bishop? Do you have any idea what kind of a man you're dealing with?"

I started smiling unconsciously. "Do you have any idea where you would be if it wasn't for Bishop? You would have been violently tortured and killed by now. I don't understand his desire to help me any more than you do, but I do know he's been a part of this when even I gave up. But believe me, I trust him a lot more than I trust you."

"Point taken, but be careful who you decide to lay with. Fleas and ticks aren't perceptive enough to know what kind of dogs they are living off."

Before I could respond, a black GMC Suburban with darkened windows and government license plates pulled in front of us, blinking the high beams before cutting off the lights. Micah got out without saying another word and went to the driver's side. When the window rolled down, Micah said something to the guy driving while pointing to the building and floor we were on. As if on cue, Bishop exited the building looking pleasantly surprised at the SUV, with Big Nasty at his side. He walked to the BMW, opened the back door, letting Big Nasty in. Big Nasty rolled himself up in a big ball taking up more than two thirds of the backseat. Bishop then proceeded to get in the driver's seat.

"Yo, podna. I told you sister was way out of our league. I don't know about this cabin shit either, man. I ain't too particular about goin' to some little hick town, 'specially when we can just check into a nice downtown suite that got room service, ESPN, and Cristal," Bishop said, cutting the engine on without turning on the lights. The engine purred softly as if it was just relaxing before being asked to explode across the road.

"Bishop, I know I owe you a lot, but do me a favor. Let's go along with Micah for the moment. I know you're as curious as I am to find out exactly where she's going with this. If she can help me find the person or persons who killed my wife, I have no choice but to follow along like a dog on a leash. I'd like to have you around just in case she starts to pull my chain in a direction I have no business going," I pleaded as gracefully as I knew how.

"Damn, dawg, does this mean ya startin' to trust my black ass?" Bishop asked, grinning, his white teeth glowing in the moonlight.

I couldn't tell if he was being his typical sarcastic self or not but I tried taking the high road. "I guess you can say that, Bishop. As I told Micah, you've stuck in this when even I gave up. You saved Micah's life tonight, not me. I was at home, asleep, after spending the whole day feeling sorry for myself. I don't understand your reasoning for doing all you've done so far, but if put in the wrong situation, I believe you'd pull me through."

"I ask myself that same question. Why am I riskin' everything I have, mainly my life, to help some bourgeois brother workin' on a death wish? The only answer I can come up with that makes any sense is I'm just an action junkie. You and Micah seem to be headin' into a bowl of shit, and I'd like to come along for the ride. Nigga ain't got too much more to do until I can start school again anyway."

"So you're going back to school, my brother? I'm sure your granma-ma is happy about that," I said with a genuine smile.

"Yeah, dawg. I figured you'd like that bit of info. 'Specially since your good word to the higher-ups helped make this a done deal. So ya see, I got a real reason for stickin' my neck out for ya black ass."

Before I could reply, Micah started toward the car and the two white guys exited the van and walked toward the building we had just left. Micah opened the door on the driver's side, even though Bishop was seated comfortably with a wide grin on his face.

"You don't expect me to sit in the back with that silly dog of yours, do you?" Micah asked, waiting for Bishop to move. "Remember I'm the one who knows where we're going."

"Baby, I know your bad ass ain't scared of my little puppy," Bishop replied laughingly as he slowly got out of the front seat. Standing face-to-face with Micah, he gently put his hand on her waist and guided her into the seat while letting his hand brush her hips and behind.

Ignoring Bishop, or at least trying to act like she was, Micah looked at me and said in her most caustic voice, "Just remember this is the asshole you feel comfortable trusting your life to."

We spent the next couple of hours getting ready for our trip. I called Gina and asked her if she could keep Ashley for a few days as we tried to sort things out. After promising Gina a little more money, she readily agreed. I think Gina was getting attached to Ashley anyway and wasn't looking forward to being in her apartment alone. I always thought of my sister as being a lonely young lady, but she swears she's happy. Bishop had a set of clothes in the trunk of his car in his Louis Vitton hanging bag and case. He called it his single man's stash. Micah called it the walking man's whore kit. I laughed at the both of them. We stopped at my house, and I threw a bag together and called my dad. I hated keeping secrets from him but I didn't feel like explaining my actions so I just told him I'd be away on business for a couple of days. We left the house finally about 4:00 A.M. and started down 285 to 75 north. Helen, Georgia, was about two hours outside of Atlanta, and I was more than ready to get the show on the road.

Micah and I settled in the backseat while Bishop drove with Big Nasty sitting on the passenger side. Bishop would reach over every now and then and stroke the dog's head while we listened to the Miles Davis classic *"Bitches Brew."* Micah said she was hungry, so we stopped at the Waffle House about a half hour outside of Atlanta. I thought it was kind of morbid but I couldn't help but think about my first date with my wife and how much fun we had.

There wasn't much conversation going on at breakfast. Bishop bought Big Nasty a couple of waffles and hamburgers after walking him around the parking lot and letting him take care of his personal business. It only took the dog about ten seconds to gulp down the waffles and hamburgers. When we got back in the car, Bishop drove, and Micah laid her head on my lap and fell into a deep sleep almost immediately. She looked more beautiful than ever lying in my lap and snoring softly. I started to feel things moving in me I hadn't felt since Andrea's death. I ran my hand through Micah's beautiful silken hair, and she moved even closer to me.

"You getting comfortable back there, huh?" Bishop asked, checking us out in his rearview mirror and grinning foolishly. "So what do you think of our lady there? You ain't falling for sister cool, are you?"

"No, Bishop, I'm not falling for anyone, especially our friend here. There are just too many unanswered questions that are associated with her. I'm not even sure that once I do get the answers I'll feel any different," I responded, shoving my emotions back into the corner where they belonged.

"I think you and sista girl make a great combination. So why don't you get comfortable back there with Ms. Playmate of the Year, and I'll get us to the secret hideout without any of our country bumpkin cops stopping us," Bishop replied, sounding like he actually cared one way or the other.

Chapter 24

Bishop woke us about an hour and a half later. The sun, rising with a deep yellow and orange glow surrounded by a beautiful haze, was just coming up over the horizon. Helen is surrounded by the impressive North Georgia mountains near the Unicoi State Park. I had visited the beautiful park on a number of occasions during high school field trips. I still remember it as a huge place with enormous trees and rolling hills.

We checked in without a hitch and were directed to a cabin about five hundred yards off the main road. It was a two-story rustic cabin built from yesterday's history with all the benefits of today's modern technology. Prefabricated logs and stones made up the walls and deck. The deck surrounded the entire building with a Jacuzzi in the back, and a great view of the mountains and the sunrise. Thick wood columns supported the deck and a thick layer of the small seashells you might see on the beach covered the base.

Bishop's car glided across the shells as they cracked and crumbled under the weight. We parked in the back, and Bishop opened his door, and Big Nasty flew out of the door and ran off into the thick oak trees that enclosed the cabin. Micah got out and stretched her body seductively then started toward the cabin door.

"Bishop, would you please control your dumb dog and try not to bring too much attention to our arrival." Then directing her attention to me and pointing to Bishop she said, "I'm going in and take a shower. Can you keep your dog under control until we can all talk?"

Before I could answer, she had already unlocked the door and gone inside, slamming the door forcefully behind her. Bishop walked up to me, grinning broadly and said, "I take back what I said earlier, boss, I think she got the wet panties for me."

I let that pass and started unloading the car with Bishop's help. The cabin was everything Micah had described and more. It opened into an enormous great room decorated in an old-time western style with rugs covering a great deal of the floor. There was a leather sofa with matching loveseat and chair on one side. A fifty-two-inch big-screen TV, stereo, cable box, and VCR were directly across from the sofa. Bishop immediately squatted in front of the television and started channel-surfing. Big Nasty strolled in and laid down next to Bishop and put his head on Bishop's thigh. He watched his master channel-surf, gazing intently at Bishop and the stations he flipped between.

I grabbed the bags he had dumped on the floor and started exploring the rest of the cabin. The kitchen was a mixture of brown and tan with a light oak kitchen table fully set for four. The stove, dishwasher, and microwave were built into the tan counter and cabinets. I dropped the bags and looked into the cabinets and found them full of food and eating utensils. The refrigerator was also stocked with fresh vegetables, fruit, meat, and drinks. I grabbed a Coke, picked up the bags, and started looking for the bedrooms. I was hoping this place had more than two bedrooms because I wasn't looking to sleep in the same room with Bishop, and I knew Micah would have me for lunch if I asked her about sleeping in the same room with her.

I could hear the shower running at the end of the hallway and Micah singing softly. I recognized the song as Anita Baker's "I Apologize" and was again amazed at Micah and her many talents. Micah's voice was so beautiful, and it took me a second to pull away from its sweet spell. I was beginning to believe that anything Micah wanted to do, she could do it better than most.

On both sides of the hallway, there were two doorways. The first one on the left-hand side was a child's bedroom with a twin-size poster bed and a bureau. The bed was covered with a pretty pink flowered bedspread. There were dolls and stuffed animals spread across the head of the bed, as well as ballet pictures with pretty little dancers in a variety of poses on each wall. The room made me feel lonely for Ashley.

I left the room feeling a little shaky and went to the one directly across from it, which was decorated exactly the opposite from the one I had just left. It was easily a boy's room. Decorated with the Atlanta Hawks basketball team paraphernalia on the full-sized bed and windows, including a big cardboard Harry the hawk mascot cutout. I dumped Bishop's bags in this room, assuming the other two doorways held at least one more bedroom.

As I started to check out the other rooms, Micah came out of the bathroom. She had a big beach towel wrapped around her and a fresh-washed look radiating from her body. Her long hair was glistening with water, and her skin was covered with water drops, and from the pleasant smell I picked up baby oil. She looked as beautiful as ever, and I felt a long-forgotten twinge in the bottom of my stomach. She was looking directly at me, and I could feel myself blushing. I hated the way my body betrayed me.

Before I could divert my eyes from her, she walked up to me, put her hands on my waist and pulled me closer to her. It felt awkward as I tried to hold my bag and keep her from pulling me into her world. I didn't want her to feel the effect she was having on me, so I tried to move but she pulled me even closer and started to kiss me on the lips. First gently and softly but building in intensity and passion. I started to feel her heartbeat mixing into mine as our tongues explored each other's mouth. I don't remember dropping my bag but my hands were empty, and they were participating in pulling her closer and deeper into me. I could feel the passion between my legs start to grow.

"I really hate to interrupt you fine folks but don't cha think you two can take that to an empty bedroom?" Bishop's grinning voice interrupted my fantasy.

I pulled away from Micah, and her towel fell to the floor. Her skin was as beautiful as I remembered from the club. She reached down slowly and picked up the towel. She didn't try to cover her body with the towel, instead slinging it over her shoulder, her eyes never once breaking contact with mine. "We will continue this later, my handsome hero. Give me about ten minutes and let's all sit down, and I'll finally tell you guys all the secrets you've both waited so patiently for."

"You've been saying that since early this morning, silly woman, and I'm tired of waiting. If you're gonna fill us in, fill us in. Personally I think you're full of shit, but you've got the wool pulled over Noah's head or is it your skirt pulled down to your ankles?" Bishop said then turned around to head back toward the TV and remote control, breaking out in a deep laugh that annoyed me more than it probably did Micah.

"I am really starting to get pissed at your friend, but maybe after we finish talking, he'll change his stripes," Micah said.

"I hope you're right, but I'm tired of being yanked around by you also, so why don't you put some clothes on and let's get this over with."

"As you wish, my hero. Just give me five minutes." And with that said, Micah kissed me softly on the cheek, turned around, and sashayed her cute round butt to her room.

Chapter 25

"I don't know where I should start but here goes nothing," Micah began. "As you've probably figured out by now, my baby sister is missing, and I plan on finding her. Darquita wrote me a cryptic letter months ago, and I haven't heard anything else from her since." Micah had slipped into a big blue-and-gray Hampton University T-shirt that obviously belonged to some man, a pair of running shorts, and some Nike running shoes. She was lying on the carpet, gazing into space, and looking at no one in particular. The room seemed so much warmer with Micah in it, or was it me who was getting warm?

"Big deal, woman, most little girls don't keep in contact with their overbearing big sisters anyway," Bishop jumped in never taking his eyes off the TV.

"Okay, dummy, let me set this up for you. My sister and I have always been close. She tells me everything and vice versa. We've never had anyone else but each other. I put her through school, and she's not a little girl, she's a grown woman," Micah continued, focusing her hard gaze directly at Bishop.

"If you consider her a grown woman, why you sweatin' her and her whereabouts? She probably laying on some beach with Prophet, getting her freak on," Bishop said.

"That's strange, too. She never mentioned having a relationship with some rapper named Prophet. And before you say something stupid, Bishop, yes we did have the kind of relationship that she could tell me anything. I've known about every boyfriend and one-night stand my sister has ever had."

"Then what happened?" I asked.

"I don't know, baby. All I know is that my sister is missing, and I want her found. I need to get back into the club. That's where all the answers are," Micah said.

"That shit ain't happening, pretty lady. Dominique had your ass killed or at least he thinks you're dead, so you definitely ain't welcomed in his club," Bishop chipped in.

"Well that's that then. I didn't want to do this but I just may have to kidnap Dominique's ass and get my answers the old-fashion way," Micah replied, looking disgusted and disappointed in this revelation.

"You ain't as smart as you act, silly woman. Dominique ain't one to travel alone, and his boys are always strapped to the nines. I don't care how bad you think you are, you ain't going to take him alive without getting yourself killed," Bishop said.

"You ain't got a better idea, so I've got to do something," Micah said.

"I never said I didn't have a better idea, woman," Bishop said with that mischievous look in his eyes again.

"Hold that thought, Bishop. Before you or I go any further, Micah still has some explaining to do. I want to know who you really are. No shortcuts, no lies. Tell me all of it or start planning your suicide," I said, looking straight into Micah's eyes.

Micah held my gaze for about fifteen seconds before getting up and walking to the glass doors and looking out at the beautiful sunset.

The view was magnificent, and I realized that it had been such a long time since I had taken the time to notice how beautiful my surroundings were. I have always liked nature and the beauty it possessed. I got up and stood next to Micah. I wanted to hold her in my arms so badly, but I just said, "Tell us all of it, please."

"There's not much that I can tell the both of you without serious repercussions to me and to you," Micah said. "But I will let you know that I used to work for our government in a highly classified position. This position was highly unique because I had the ability to be above and beyond the laws that the general Joe on the street had to abide by."

"Storybook time," Bishop said barely audible to Micah or me.

"Believe what you want but I don't have to prove myself to you or anyone else. I am who I am. I've been asked to participate in actions in more foreign countries than I'd care to remember. Our government trained me to do the work that the general public finds squeamish, the jobs you don't want showing up on your nightly news. But I left all of that so that I can find my sister, and I promise you that there is no limit to the drama I'll create to do just that."

"Were the guys who showed up last night part of the group you used to work for?" I asked.

"They were friends who owed me a couple of favors. I tend to have a great number of acquaintances who for one reason or another believe that I am worth the extra effort," Micah replied with a smile.

"So is that it?" Bishop asked.

"What else do you want explained?" Micah asked.

"Do you know who and why these guys are after you?" I asked, realizing immediately that I knew as much about that as she did.

"They were after me because I was getting too close to their little moneymaking paradise, but they just don't understand. I don't give a fuck about their play things, I just want my sister," Micah said.

"I believe your sister and her rapper boyfriend, Prophet, are directly connected to Dominique's continued success. But if you look at me like you look at my boy here," Bishop continued, pointing to me, "I'll tell you a surefired way we can get back into the club and start some more drama."

"How about you get us back into the club, and I promise not to kick your ass," Micah said softly.

"Well since you put it that way, beautiful. I got a sister who would love to spend her days and nights butt naked while enjoying the company of other beautiful naked women," Bishop replied with that mischievous look in his eyes.

"One of your old housewife hookers ain't got nothing to do for the next couple of weeks?" Micah asked nastily.

"You need to be nice to me and mine, woman. I still don't know how you seem to know so much about me. You just met me yesterday."

"Nigga, please. You didn't think I would remember your ugly-ass face and ponytail from the club. You were chasing my ass all over the city for a couple of days. I just didn't know how you were connected to this mess."

"Damn, I thought I was deep undercover. But your ass is so fine, I'm sure I just lost a little focus. But you just gained some brownie points because ain't nobody ever scooped me when I didn't want to be scooped," Bishop said slightly agitated at Micah's heads-up on him.

"Bishop, I've told you before your ass ain't that good. But if you can get one of your hookers into the club, I'll owe you a big one," Micah replied reluctantly.

"My baby ain't a hooker. She's the only bitch that could carry my nine and my bank book," Bishop said, staring directly into Micah's eyes and looking even more aggravated than before.

"Damn, Bishop, is Bitch her first or last name?" Micah asked in her most innocent voice.

"Alright both of you. Let it go," I interrupted. "Bishop, how soon can you get this rolling?"

"I'll give her a call in a minute and see if I can get her to meet us here. She'll come, and she'll do what I ask of her but she's going to want to know the whole deal. Is that a problem for you, super-sleuth?" Bishop asked, directing the question to Micah.

"Like I said before, Bishop, I'll do anything to get my sister back, including dealing with you and yours," Micah said.

"Okay, then it's settled. While you set that up, Bishop, do you mind holding down the fort? I see Micah has her running stuff, and I saw a running trail on our way up. Do you mind if I work out with you, Micah?"

"Baby, if that's what it takes for me to get you alone, we can run up this whole damn mountain," Micah said with exaggerated flourish.

Chapter 26

It only took me about five minutes to throw on some shorts and running shoes, and when I got outside Micah was already in the middle of her stretching routine. She had dropped the Hampton University T-shirt and replaced it with a form-fitting Lycra sleeveless running top. I started my stretching routine and within ten minutes, we were running at an easy pace up the mountain path.

Micah ran like a seasoned athlete, but I was not surprised. She was so beautiful and fine even here and now, sweating and pushing her body. Her look was intense and dedicated to the event. Her stride was long and graceful on this rugged mountain trail. Her breathing was calculated and strong, and I tried my best to match her stride for stride. I was amazed that I was able to keep pace with her since running wasn't my strong suit. But I guess that my competitive spirit was stoked at the thought of chasing her fine sculpted body up this hill, or was that my manly spirit?

Running at a medium pace we made it to the top of the slope in about twenty minutes. Micah stopped with her hands on her hips to catch her breath, and I welcomed the needed break also. This clear, thinner air made the trip a little harder, but I loved the rush in my chest the workout caused. The view up there was magnificent. The beginning of fall was starting to take an effect on the surrounding trees, changing the leaves to a kaleidoscope of vibrant colors that were scattered throughout the trees as well as the forest floor.

"Can I ask you a question, Noah?" Micah asked.

"Sure," I replied, lowering myself to the ground and sitting with my legs stretched out completely in front of me as my torso leaned forward, my hands touching my toes.

"What was it about your wife that makes you so crazy about finding her killer?" Micah asked after sitting Indian-style.

"I could ask you the same thing about your desire to find your sister, but I'm not in a confrontational mood right now. And I really don't know how to answer your question," I replied.

"Come on, you can do better than that," Micah pushed.

I thought about it for a minute. I knew the answer, and I knew the words that described it perfectly, but for some reason I didn't want to share it. After about a minute I gave in and said, "*We flowed.*"

Micah smiled, and I knew what she was going to ask before she asked so I continued.

"I can't describe the way we lived together any better than that. In fact it was Andrea who first coined the phrase. While we were driving through Atlanta to enjoy one of our favorite sports – *eating* - I asked her to explain what she meant by that, and she looked at me like I was asking her why the sun rose in the east and set in the west." I smiled at the memory of Andrea saying those words for the first time.

"We flowed because it was the natural order of things. It was the little things, mainly. Driving down the road listening to our favorite jazz channel and having her reach over and softly run her hand over my chest. She always made me feel like a man. I loved waking her up in the morning with breakfast in bed, complete with coffee and juice and her favorite section of the newspaper and was always amused when she proclaimed that she couldn't taste a drop of the food until she tinkled. Most mornings we arose with the sun to stretch and meditate together before facing the world. Do you know what it feels like to have your significant other call you in the middle of a busy day just to say she's downstairs with a picnic basket and would love to have your company for lunch?" I asked, looking directly into Micah's eyes, feeling flushed.

"No, Noah, I've never had the love you and your wife shared."

"Then I feel sorry for you. I loved my wife fiercely. I loved telling her that there would never be a battle that she would have to fight on her own. We never felt smothered when we spent every moment together, or alone when we weren't together. I loved being in the house and still feeling complete even though she was nowhere to be found. Her presence, her being, her *flow* was always there," I said, feeling naked at the way I had bared my soul to this woman who I still knew so little about, but who also made my body feel alive again when I looked at her.

"Believe it or not, I dream of loving a man that way one day but only if he has the same passion for me," Micah added, looking off into the fading sun.

"I wish you luck. I never really believed in the love Andrea and I shared before it happened, but now there is no way I could ever love any less."

"You don't seem surprised by my desire to be madly in love one day, Noah. I thought my bad-ass independent-sister act was working well."

"I believe your bad-ass act. I think you are a ruthless, cold woman who can kill at the drop of a hat. You scare me, and I think your desire to be madly in love is what's fake," I replied.

"Damn, Noah, can you please take the knife out of my chest. That was just plain mean," Micah replied, standing and turning her back to me. "I'm trying to open up here, and you're hurting a sister. I can't change the way I have lived or the decisions I've made as far as my career is concerned. But, I am still a human being with all of the emotional baggage and dreams that most people have."

"Okay. I apologize. But it doesn't change the facts about you or the life that you've lived. I need you to help me through my drama and I think you are going to need me before this is over with, but I am still very scared of the life you live."

"But you trust Bishop?" Micah spitted bitterly.

"Where does this anger come from toward Bishop, Micah? Is there something about Bishop and you that I don't know?" I asked.

"No, Noah, there isn't. I just don't trust him, and I don't think you should either. He is from the bottom of the barrel, and all he's going to do is drag you down with him. But more than that, you should ask Bishop about his real relationship with Dominique," Micah continued.

"What are you talking about, Micah?"

"Bishop knows more about Dominique than he's letting on, honey, and I'll leave that at that," Micah shouted over her shoulder as she started running down the hill back toward the cabin.

I started to go after her, but I figured I needed a break now. Micah was so damn mysterious. She expected me to trust her explicitly, but she expected me to be wary of Bishop. But if it weren't for Bishop, she would be dead, and I wouldn't be as close as I was to finding my wife's killer. What in the hell did she mean by Bishop's relationship to Dominique? Why did the two people to whom I have entrusted my future have secrets and hate? And how did my wife's murder fit in to all of this?

Damn. I was getting a headache.

Chapter 27

Bishop's friend showed up just after dinner. Micah and I had showered separately, and were in the middle of a heated argument on the necessity of race-based scholarships at predominately black schools for white kids when the woman knocked at the door.

The first thing I noticed when Bishop let her in was the way their eyes met, and they both seemed to forget anyone else was in the room. They held each other closely for quite a while, and then Bishop started laughing.

"Damn. Baby, I missed you," Bishop said, holding her at arm's length and allowing his eyes to completely envelope her physical presence without letting her go.

"I missed you, too, lover. Why don't you introduce me to your friends?" Mia replied, turning toward us.

"Baby, I never said that they were my friends, but anyway, Mia this is Noah, and the mean-looking sister to his right is

Micah," Bishop said, pointing at each of us as he called our name but never taking his eyes off Mia.

Mia was striking in her own unique way. She wore stunning burnt- red-shoulder length dreadlocs. Her cheekbones were distinct, and they fit her beautiful pearly smiling face. She only stood about five feet tall, but the three-inch purple-and-black pumps she wore accented her finely sculpted legs. She was wearing a pair of black stonewashed Gap jeans and a tight-fitting purple top. Her breasts filled out every inch of the shirt, and I wondered how her small frame handled the weight of them. Don't get me wrong, they weren't of the Dolly Parton magnitude, but they were quite a handful. Her voice was light and childlike.

Mia walked over to me and shook my hand while taking me in from top to bottom as a man would a woman who he found physically attractive. Her hand was small and soft.

"So you're the head nigga in charge," Mia whispered, as she looked me dead in the eyes. "Bishop told me a lot about you and your situation when he called, and I couldn't wait to get here and see what kind of man would go through all this drama for the love of a woman. You do your brothers proud, and if I had a man like you in my life, I probably wouldn't like my sisters as much as I do."

Before I could comment, she let go of my hand and walked to within inches of Micah's face. Her breasts seemed to touch Micah's upper stomach as she looked up into her eyes. "And you must be Super Bitch. Why don't you give a sister a hug, Micah?" Mia said cutely as she put her arms around Micah's waist and pulled her close.

Micah smiled broadly and followed directions to the T, bending down slightly and wrapping her arms around Mia's shoulders.

They held this position for a couple of seconds before Micah let her go and just stared down at this little woman with the beautiful breasts.

"Bishop, why didn't you tell us your lady friend was a dyke? And, baby, how long have you been growing those beautiful dreadlocs? They are exquisite," Micah said in her most polite voice.

"My baby ain't gay. She just likes life and all of the beautiful things life has to offer," Bishop replied as he took a seat on the sofa.

Mia walked over to the sofa where Bishop was sitting, kicking off her shoes on the way and cuddled up next to him.

"Baby, don't mind my big brother wanna-be. He's still in denial. Bishop figures can't no woman be gay with him around. But if you want to stay in my good graces, please refer to my locs as locs. They are definitely not dreadful so the white man's description ain't necessary."

"Explain to me what the white man has to do with me calling your locs, dreadlocs?" Micah asked, taking a seat on the floor as I grabbed a chair.

"Oh, shit. Y'all done asked for it now. This woman loves talking about her 'mature' locs and the history behind them," Bishop replied, smiling at the forthcoming conversation.

Mia turned in his lap and punched him hard on his arm, then turned back to us.

"This nigga would love to have a headful of locs but his shit's too wavy. And I don't like to embellish on my beautiful mature locs," Mia said, sitting up and running her hands through her hair. "I resent the word *dreadlocs* and the history lesson that goes with it. Does anyone here besides Bishop know the real history behind the word *dreadlocs*?"

Before anyone could respond, she continued the lesson. "When we were being shipped like cattle from the homeland to America a funny thing happened on the way. When we first arrived on shore and were taken out of the ship's dark hellish hole by our pale blond captors, the sight of our hair of all things took them aback. It didn't bother them that most of us were sick and skeletal, covered with vomit, shit, and piss. During the trip, we learned to twist and groom our hair as it grew through the long nightmare we were living at that time. We called them locs but the white devil called them dreadful. So dreadlocs was born. Or at least that's the story I was told by my loctician when I decided to change to my current hairstyle. I've heard many variations of the origin of this style and the name; so don't hold me to this view. But, hold me to the fact that dreadlocs just doesn't describe my hairstyle."

"Damn, I didn't know that. And since I do like the sound of locs, locs it is, my little sister," Micah said, sounding like Mia was now her best friend.

"Okay. Enough with the history lesson. Let's talk about how we gon' get this drama over with. How do you want to play this, boss, now that you got the A team on your side?" Bishop jumped in, directing his question to me.

"Good question, Bishop. But, I'd be lying if I told you I had half a clue as to what direction we should pursue next," I answered, feeling dumber and dumber by the minute.

"Then let's put together a plan of action. I say we just go in, let me put this nine up Dominique's ass, and we'll get all of the answers to all of our combined questions," Micah said.

"Yeah, right. Dominique's dawgs would have loaded your ass with hollow points before you ever got close enough to smell his cologne," Bishop chimed in.

"Straight out violence won't get me to the head guy, nor will that help us find your sister, Micah. I think I've got a better idea. What about a three-angle attack," I jumped in, feeling nervous at the thought of trying to give these seasoned street veterans ideas.

"Run it by us, love, I'm all ears," Mia said before anyone else could say anything.

"Well it all starts with you, Mia. We need someone to work the club and let us know what's happening. I know this is a lot for a relative stranger to ask of you, but would you mind working in the club as a waitress and keeping an eye out for me?" I asked.

"Umm. Let me think this out. Do I mind watching beautiful naked women getting in and out of their clothes? Do I mind having silly, immature, midget-dick, horny men give me all of their money for just a peek of my stuff? Damn, I think you've just convinced me to be a stripper, hell with being a waitress," Mia said gleefully.

"Are you okay with that, Bishop?" Micah asked, trying to look innocent.

Before Bishop could answer, Mia jumped in, directing her cold response to Micah. "Bishop is my nigga, and he knows I got his back at all times. He also recognizes that I run my own life, so use someone else to fuck with his mind and leave me out of your silly-ass games, bitch."

"Damn, I wonder if that's Ms. Bitch or simply bitch?" Bishop asked, reminding Micah of her earlier comment.

"You two are made for each other," Micah responded, looking disappointed at her inability to get to Bishop. "What do you want me to do, Noah? Everyone around Dominique will be looking out for me, but I need to be in this."

"I want you to be invisible, Micah. You and Bishop both. Invisible enough to follow Dominique all over this city without him or his boys picking up a scent of either of you. I want to know his routine better than he does. If you and Bishop can keep the hostilities down between the two of you, I think we can figure out at least some of his moves before he actually makes them," I said.

Micah stared harshly at Bishop but she didn't balk at the direction I wanted her to go, and Bishop responded by smiling brightly.

"Micah, let me ask you a question. Have you ever tried to bug Dominique's office?" I asked, feeling the flow as this all seemed to come together for me.

"I considered it, but Dominique's goons always had their eyes on me. I can get the most sophisticated bugs but I just couldn't get close enough to his shit to bug it," Micah replied, looking a little dejected at the thought of her not being able to do something she wanted.

"Girl, that ain't no problem. I'm sure Bishop can get into any part of that building without anyone ever knowing he was there," Mia said as we all sat there looking dumb-founded at Bishop.

"Damn girl, do you have to let everyone know everything," Bishop whispered, barely audible to the rest of us as he pushed her away and started toward the door.

"Hold on, dawg. You got something to tell us?" I asked, standing up and moving toward him as my mind took me back to the comment Micah had made earlier about Bishop knowing more about Dominique and the club than he was letting on.

"Yeah, there's more. I used to own the club before I sold it to Dominique and his group," Bishop replied. Before I could form all of the questions that rushed into my head, he added, "And I have nothing else to say on the matter. I've still got keys if their cheap asses haven't changed all of the locks, and I'll get

Micah and her bugs in, but don't ask for any other answers. That was a part of my life I left a long time ago." And with that said Bishop got up and headed out the door.

Chapter 28

I started not to follow Bishop but this drama was getting even more stupid, minute by minute, so I needed to know it all. I grabbed my coat and Bishop's off the sofa and started for the door after him. Micah stood to follow. I turned to her and said, "Give me a minute with him, Micah. It'll be hard enough to get him to talk to me without you and your smart comments backing everything up."

"Damn, am I really that bad?" Micah asked ingeniously as she turned around and sat back down.

It didn't take me long to find Bishop since he was propped up against the porch rail, seemingly waiting for me. I tossed Bishop his coat and asked, "You want to take a walk and talk this out, Bishop?"

Bishop didn't say anything as he slipped on his coat and headed down the stairs. I followed, putting into play one of my greatest negotiating tactics I just stayed quiet. Just shutting up and being patient is a simple but effective tactic when you need someone to talk to you. One of my marketing professors loved to remind us that a person can't accept a deal unless you shut up long enough for him to say yes.

Bishop started down the only path leading from the cabin and farther into the forest. The posted signs said that the path we were following would take us to Champagne Falls. The surrounding area was absolutely beautiful, and the farther we walked into the forest, the more striking the natural scenery became. During my run with Micah, I was able to enjoy the area but taking this slow, leisurely walk gave me more time to appreciate God's beauty. We arrived at the falls after about thirty minutes of silent revelry. The falls, which were about sixty feet high, flowed gently down the massive cliff. The water was so crystal clear that you could see the colored stones behind the running water. The trees, which grew above the basin and on the ground surrounding the stream, were full of life. The birds sang and flew at leisure. There were animal tracks all over the soft ground but I had no idea what tracks belonged to what kind of animal. I just hoped none of them wanted to eat me for dinner.

Bishop stared at the falls in awe, and I was surprised to see the delight in his eyes. He walked along the stream, taking in the countryside the same way that I guess I did. As much as I'd like to deny it, we both enjoyed so much of life. It also dawned on me that from my own responses to Bishop that I, too, had a very messed-up view of the man. Was it so hard for me to believe that just because Bishop had lived the life that he had that he was incapable of enjoying nature and its beauty as I would? Why could I believe and not question Micah's love for life when I knew she'd been as cruel as Bishop? Was I normal folk with all of the subconscious bigotry that Bishop accused everyone else of having?

We took in this scenery in silence for about ten minutes before Bishop decided to open his mouth.

"You think you know about my past, don't you?"

"I know what little you've told me and the stuff I've read," I answered honestly.

"So much more to me and my world, dawg, than any piece of paper could tell you. Me trying to even explain my shit to you is so fucked up to start with. You and your Cosby life, me and my street shit, it can't get no more different. But, my escape from that life wasn't easy, and I really can't be sure I've actually put that drama behind me. As they say in the hood, the game keeps calling my name."

"Do you really believe that I can't feel you on this, Bishop, or that the game can get to you all the way up here?" I asked, waving my hand around.

"It ain't about you feeling me, Noah. Even you know we can't run away from the world we don't live in just because we change addresses. I lived this life. I walked the walk and talked the talk. I've had to be judge, jury, and executioner on the street but I didn't ask for this shit. I was born into it, without my permission. You can't buy a gun without a permit or drive a car without a license but any two fools can fuck and make a baby. Ten seconds of passion if they're lucky, and some poor bastard's cursed for life."

"Do you know what's the worse part of being born poor?" Bishop continued.

"No, I don't, Bishop," I said, knowing that any other answer would be empty words to Bishop's ears.

"It's never being able to forget where you came from or what it's like, even if you've got a bank full of money or are living large and sleeping on satin sheets in your king-size bed. As much as my gran-mama wanted to make things right for us, she couldn't grow money in her garden. Or really provide for my sister and me, and with my mom stealing and selling anything of value to support her habit, it didn't help our situation, either. I find it so funny when people who have money speak so eloquently about how money isn't so important. The spoiled bourgeois college kids I use to put up with in school are so quick to jump into their brand-new cars wearing their expensive clothes and then brag about how hard they have it. But this ain't what ya came out here for, is it?"

"I don't know why I came out here, Bishop. For reasons I can't quite explain, I do trust you. I do believe you've got my back, but I can't justify your actions. I don't know why you're hanging with this. I knew there was probably more to it than you just wanting a little action, a little drama to spice up the day. But I never thought there was a connection between Dominique and you, which was stupid on my part. The way Detective Harris put us together should have sent off bells ringing in my head."

"Fuck that old man. I'm in this game for my reasons, not his guilty conscious. I'm the one with the truly guilty conscious here anyway," Bishop spitted out.

"Bishop, there are a lot of people out here who would have a hard time picturing you with a conscious, especially a guilty one."

"Again, fuck people. People have no idea about my life. Past, present, or future. Regular folk think playas like me want to play this stupid game. They believe we like being born into total poverty where the rats are your pets. They believe we want to beg for food every day, attend schools where you can graduate without learning how to write your own name, wake up every day to gunfire and death, rape and murder. People stupid! Especially, everyday folk. One reason I liked you from the start was that you a humble nigger. Born with a foundation that very few of us get a chance to have but never flaunting it. Thin line between jealousy and respect, dawg. I respect you but we still from different sides of the track. But the main reason I'm hanging is because I want some thug revenge."

"What are you talking about, Bishop?"

"I want to legally fuck Dominique. I want to pay him back for screwing me and mine. He's the reason my nigga was tortured and killed. That's how he got my club and my spot in the game. I didn't give a damn about the niche I laid in the field but Delmar was my nigga. We were joined at the hip and the heart. We downed forties together, we popped condoms together. Wasn't nuthin' I wouldn't do for that nigga and vice versa. He saved my life when I was about ten, and I could never do enough to pay him back, but he wasn't as smart as I was, so he followed while I lead."

"So are you saying this is all about revenge?" I asked, accepting that reason better than relying on Bishop's altruistic nature.

"Revenge and a chance for me to make up for my own stupidity."

"Explain."

"Have you ever read the book *The Art of War?*"

"By Sun Tzu."

"Yeah. I ran my business by that Chinese nigga's words. I give it all the credit for my street shit and my planning to leave that drama behind me for a legit life. Ruthless as my business could be, it was my way to get ahead without any unnecessary bloodshed. One of his cardinal rules is to know your enemy. I knew everything about Dominique. His wants, his needs, the way he ran his business, the fact that he loved the sound of his own voice and had an unnecessary need to be brutal. Since I knew all of this I should have never left Delmar alone to handle my business and Dominique. It was just a matter of time before Dominique got greedy and decided to go after Delmar. My stupid mistake, but I needed to get out of the game."

"Bishop, by your own words you're no better than Dominique, even though you've supposedly gotten out of the game. So what's the difference? Just because you've read a couple of books and supposedly didn't get any joy out of the things you've done, it's supposed to be all good? What gives you the right to even think about trying to get even with someone who's no more than a mirror image of you?"

"Damn dawg. Don't hate the playa, hate the game. Again, like I told you before, I didn't ask for this shit, I was born into it. What are any of us supposed to do? Starve? Work at Burger King for the rest of our lives? But that shit don't matter anyway. Dominique sic'd his boys on Delmar when we had a deal, then he pinned it on me. I ain't taking this shit lying down, and Detective Dick knew this. He introduced you to me hoping that I could legitimately take out Dominique, with a subtle assist from you. I'm sure Micah was a wild card he didn't count on in this silly equation, but it's still all good."

"So are you saying that you're in this to win it with no more secrets?"

"We all got secrets, nigga. But we in this together, you, me, and super bitch. And believe me, my secrets ain't no different from Micah's. When you gonna give in and hit that, dawg? She feigning for your ass, and she ain't ashamed to show it."

"Now, you really reaching, Bishop," I said, recognizing his effort to change the subject and him wanting me to go along with it. I got what I needed from Bishop, which was his commitment to finishing this drama, and I realized that I wasn't going to get him to open up any more than he wanted to.

"Noah, I know you loved the piss out of your wife, but remember she's not here anymore. She's dead, and you've got to go on with your life. I don't know how long you plan to mourn for her but you still a hard-leg nigga with needs. Push it aside if you want but that lust never goes away. And I don't want you fucking off in lala land daydreaming about some shit when you supposed to be watching my back."

"So you're worried that I'm not going to have your back when you, in your rage, are trying to break Dominique's neck because you sacrificed your best friend for your freedom?"

"No, nigga. I'm worried about Micah thinking about that throbbing feeling between her legs when I need her to have my back and yours. Man, you need to handle that sista because if I had the opportunity to even smell that salad, I would be on top of the world or should I say on top of her."

"What are you going to do to Dominique, Bishop?" I asked already knowing the answer but wanting to change the subject.

"Does it matter, nigga? That's between the two of us. Our drama. Our thug life. But you can bet your life that he will suffer for a long time. Payback is a bitch, especially from me. You entertain your own personal revenge, and I'll more than handle mine."

Chapter 29

We all spent a peaceful night in the cabin and started home the next morning. Bishop figured Sunday would be the best day to go in and bug Dominique's club. Micah wasn't as sure about that so they argued back and forth on when was the best time, but we finally agreed to do it right before dusk with Micah promising a little surprise for us to assure our chances of not being interrupted. Mia was eager to get home and prepare for her "getting naked" interview so she was on her way back to Atlanta as soon as the sun rose. With that settled, I headed straight for my sister's house so that I could spend the whole day with my daughter and put up with my sister.

Gina lived in a very nice apartment near midtown in the heart of Atlanta. She loved the closeness to downtown Atlanta and her job, and of course some of the best stores and restaurants the city had to offer were nearby. Being spoiled seemed to be a mold for everyone in our family. Andrea always teased me about how spoiled I was even though she loved reminding me that the reason she was spoiled was because of me. The spoiled spoiling the spoiled. Gina is no different.

I got there around ten and Gina seemed a little bothered when she saw it was me at her door.

"Don't look so disappointed, little sister. Were you expecting someone else?" I asked, searching the room for Ashley.

Gina's apartment was a small studio with a simple but expensive-looking floor plan. The entrance opened into a nice-size living and eating area covered with very nice oak floors, while the modern kitchen and bathrooms had marble. She had a small garden patio outside the window, which faced Peachtree Street. There was one other room off the bedroom that she turned into an ample office, complete with a computer system, forty-two-inch-color TV, stereo system, and a StairMaster that she never used. The TV was on its usual channel, the Food Network, even though Gina never cooked anything worth eating.

"Stop looking around for Ashley like I've sold her to the highest bidder. She's in my bedroom, and I was just about to change her and give her a bottle. Would you like to do both, or better yet, give her a bath?" Gina said sarcastically, heading for her bedroom with me close behind.

"A bath it is. You smell like you need one, too," I said jokingly, smiling from ear to ear as I spotted Ashley, staring at the lights and blowing bubbles while lying in the middle of the Gina's king-size bed surrounded by six fluffy pillows.

I jumped on the bed and grabbed my princess rolling onto my back and holding her on my chest. Ashley has a beautiful smile and eyes that make me believe that she's been here in another lifetime. I love it when people comment on how Ashley looks like her mother or me. I think she looks like ET or a chubby Chinese Buddha. Today though, she does look just like her mother, and the hurt I feel is overwhelming. Since Andrea's death, it seems like all I do is go from one extreme to the other, a roller coaster of emotions. Seeing my daughter and holding her dribbling face in my hands also fills an emptiness in me I can never explain.

"Hey, stop daydreaming, doughnuthead. Are you going to give Ashley a well- deserved bath or not?" Gina asked from the doorway, letting me enjoy my moment.

"Of course I am, little sister, but I hope you take one, too," I replied, standing up and walking to the kitchen sink while pushing playfully past Gina.

"Look, Goofy, if I need a bath, it's because your little brat's been spitting up on me all day. I call her my SES girl."

"Okay, I'll bite. Exactly what does SES mean?" I asked, knowing I was stepping into some of Gina's silly stuff.

"All your little princess does is sleep, eat, and shit. SES."

"What do you expect from my little princess? Her serving you breakfast in bed?" I asked as I grabbed Ashley's baby tub off the counter and started to run her water. Gina had all of Ashley's stuff lined up over the double sink, baby tub, mild soap, little wash cloths, baby oil and powder, some baby wipes, and diapers.

"I've got enough trouble making my own breakfast. Would you like some raisin toast and coffee?" Gina asked as she grabbed a half-finished loaf of raisin bread off the refrigerator and popped a couple of slices into the toaster before I could answer. She then grabbed a cup and saucer from the cabinet and poured herself some coffee.

"I've eaten already, and I've had your coffee before. I want to live a little longer if that's okay with you," I said, ignoring the snide look on her face and beginning to undress Ashley. It's amazing that I can still easily hold her in one hand. After filling the little tub halfway, I turned off the water and placed Ashley face up in it. She tried to cry lightly but she stopped as soon as I started to wash her. Three seconds after I began she started to giggle lightly while trying to grab the towel with one hand and splash the water with the other. After finishing with her hair and face, I wrapped her in a big towel and dried her off. Gina left the room and came back in with a matching flowered set for me to dress Ashley in. I massaged a little baby oil all over her tiny body before powdering her down and dressing her.

"Do you have any plans for today," I asked Gina as I headed to the sofa to feed Ashley the bottle of milk Gina had prepared. Ashley grabbed the bottle greedily and started gulping down the milk. She locked on to my eyes, and it seemed as if she was touching my soul. It's amazing that such a small person with no way of forming words could express so much with just a look.

At moments like that I always wondered how any parent, male or female, married or unmarried, could walk away from his or her offspring without so much as a hiccup. I have a couple of friends who've decided for whatever reasons to just stop seeing their children. One of them reminds me of the enormous burden he's under just to pay child support, and he says he has no time for "gimme" visits. He calls them gimme visits because he swears when he goes to see his kids all he hears about is the things they need and don't have and how Mom wants him to buy the kids this or that. Another deadbeat dad I know complains about how he never asked this woman to have his child, and how he even offered to pay for an abortion but Moms knew he was making a pretty good penny and like she said, "She just wanted to have a baby, no matter who the daddy is." Like I said, I just don't understand. No matter the cost or the sacrifice, if you are blessed with a child of your own making, nothing should keep you from handling your business.

"Earth to Noah, Earth to Noah."

"Sorry, Gina. Just got lost there for a minute. Did you answer my question?"

"Yes, I did but I'll answer it again. I have nothing planned except for staying at home, paying some bills online, and minding your little brat."

"Cool. I'm hoping this will be over soon so that Ashley and I can go back home and try to put our lives back together."

"Noah, I know I'm just your little sister but I'd love to know exactly what the hell you're trying to accomplish here. Dad told me that you're running all over the city playing private dick. You've got the old man worried silly."

"What has he told you about my situation?"

"Stupid question, Noah. You know Daddy ain't one for talking, especially when it comes to other folks' business. You tell me everything I need to know."

The details rolled off my tongue easier than I thought they would, and before I knew it, I had told her everything, sorting through all of the details as I conveyed them to her. I also found myself riding the emotional roller coaster of drama that had taken over my life.

Gina listened intently, and Ashley was quiet through the whole conversation. Every now and then Gina would ask for clarification on some facts or look at me like I was out of my mind, especially when I told her about Micah.

"Damn, big brother, you always attracting the aggressive super stud sisters. She sounds just like Andrea. What are you going to do about this one, marry her, too?" Gina asked, sounding as if me marrying Micah was a real option.

"No, fool. I just buried my wife a couple of months ago and the last thing on my mind is the thought of me getting serious about anybody."

"To hell with getting serious with super chick. How about you just getting yourself a little bit? Sister seems to want to give it to you anyway, and maybe that's what it'll take to bring you back down to reality before you go out here and get yourself killed by some crazy drug dealer," Gina said sounding like she truly cared. If it weren't for the comment about me getting a little bit, I'd think she was actually concerned.

"Like I said earlier, I just buried Andrea. Sex is the last thing on my mind. Now, getting back to reality, can you continue to watch Ashley for me? Dad wants Ashley back at his house tomorrow, so can you keep her here tonight and drop her off at Pop's tomorrow."

"It's going to cost you, big brother," Gina answered, flashing that "I can always use more money" grin and sticking out her hand.

"Put your begging hand down, silly. Let me just enjoy this moment with my daughter for a minute, before you bribe me out of another dollar," I tell Gina as I watch my daughter sleeping peacefully in my arms. Its times like this, I really begin to understand just how much I'm missing, trying to play catch the bad guy. But, it also brings to point clearly, what these bastards have taken away from my daughter and I. Ashley will never be able to fall asleep in her mothers' arms. For this alone they've got to pay.

Chapter 30

Bishop picked me up at my house, and we met Micah a couple of blocks away from Dominique's club in front of one of the fast-food restaurants lining the block.

She was sitting in a bronze Saab convertible with the top down even though it was a little chilly out. A matching bronze scarf adorned her head, which complimented the lighter color bronze pantsuit that covered her perfectly shaped body.

Bishop pulled up next to Micah so that she and I were facing each other.

"You ready to do this, Micah?" I asked, not knowing for sure if I was ready for whatever we were about to get into.

"Baby, you know I'm always ready, but let's wait about ten more minutes. I've got a little help coming," Micah answered with a big knowing grin spreading across her face.

Bishop started to say something stupid but before he could utter one word, Micah pointed to a set of utility trucks lumbering down the street. Micah kicked her car into gear and followed them. Bishop didn't wait for me to say a word as he pulled in right behind Micah. We drove like this until we got to the block where Dominique's club was located. As the lead truck waved us by, we followed the second truck farther down the street. Blocking the road from any oncoming traffic, the driver and his partner in the lead truck got out, and started directing traffic down an alternate street.

Micah pulled into Amazon's empty, unlocked parking lot with us close behind. The second utility truck stopped at the end of the street and repeated the performance of the first truck. Micah had effectively shut down the entire street. We all piled out of the cars, with Bishop leading us to the backside of the club.

"How you boys like that for privacy?" Micah asked seemingly directing the question right at Bishop. She had a small black box, no bigger than an earring case in one hand that I assumed held the bugs that we planned on leaving in Dominique's club.

"You asking me, Micah? You should know by now I got nothing but love for your super-agent ass. You been pulling rabbits out the hat from day one. But remember, yo ass needed us to get ya this close. So wipe that cocky-ass smile off your face and let's go see if my keys still work."

Micah, never one for being anything less than cocky, grabbed my arm and still smiling broadly followed Bishop's lead. "By the way, my friends out front can only give us about twenty minutes, so your keys better work, nigga," Micah added viciously.

Bishop turned around and flashed his stupid smile at Micah and said seriously, "Did you call me a *nigga* or a *nigger*? Because nigga shows me nothing but love but if you call me a nigger, I'd have to take that shit a lot more serious, sista girl."

Micah, ignoring Bishop, turned her back to him and continued for the door. "Bishop, I understand the difference between nigga and nigger, but I must admit I'm surprised you know the difference. And as much as I hate your ass, I would never disrespect even you by calling you a nigger even though most white folks would feel right at home calling you just that. You do fit the profile."

Bishop didn't reply verbally, but his smile got even larger. I must admit I didn't have a clue about the difference between one and the other. Nigga or nigger, they both held negative connotations to me but I guess to Bishop and Micah the difference was obvious. All I could see was two super fools having a philosophical discussion on the proper way to use *nigga*. This must be a dream. Micah must have seen the confusion on my face because she stopped long enough to say, "Noah, when you call one of your friends a nigga, does it leave a bad taste in your mouth?"

"You know the answer to that already, Micah. I have never used the word with any of my friends in a negative way. But I see the difference now. *Nigger* is the label white people used on us but *nigga* is the mutated word we use to show friendship and love, true?"

"And you wonder why I got a thing for you, handsome," Micah answered as she pulled me to the door where Bishop was trying his keys.

The door had two padlocks and two deadbolts. Bishop's keys worked on all four of them, and we were inside in no time.

Micah was directly behind me, and Bishop was leading the way. The hallway was well-lit, even though no one was there. Bishop led us down the hall and into the first room on the right. That door was locked also with a Do Not Enter sign taped on it. Bishop fished out another key and opened that deadbolt lock also.

Micah jumped ahead of both of us once the door was opened and went directly to the metal desk facing the door.

"I've only been in here a couple of times, but the bugs I've got are going to love this office," Micah said gleefully. She reminded me of a child who just got the lock opened on a cookie jar.

"Where and how many, Micah?" Bishop asked, walking around the office as if he was seeing an old friend again for the first time in years.

"One bug under the desk is all that we need," Micah answered as she took a seat behind the desk and opened her little box, pulling out a small round plastic-and-metal contraption. She dropped to her knees and disappeared. In no time at all, Micah came back up smiling. "Done, super sleuths! Let's get the hell out of here."

"Hold on, Agent 009. This isn't Dominique's main office, because it wasn't mine," Bishop whispered hoarsely as he ran his hands along the wall, which was covered with pictures and plaques.

"What the hell are you talking about, Bishop?" Micah asked, stopping in her tracks and giving him a crazy look.

Bishop didn't say anything as he continued to run his hands along the wall as if he was looking for something neither Micah nor I could see. But, before Micah or I could figure out what was going on, Bishop's hand seemed to grab an invisible latch that I heard a click. The wall immediately slid away to reveal another room. This room was about the same size as the office we were in now, but it didn't have any office furniture in it. Instead, the room was furnished with a king-size canopy bed, mirrors on three of the walls and the ceiling, a shower surrounded by glass on all four sides, an armoire, and a huge leather chair. On the one wall without the mirrors was a big-screen TV, VCR, and stereo system.

In the far corner of the same wall was a professional video camera, tripod, and assorted lights.

Before I could say a word, Bishop said "damn" and Micah started laughing, adding, "I always wondered what happened to all the little bimbos and their pimps when they came in here and disappeared for hours at a time."

I didn't know what to say so I went to the armoire and opened it. Inside was an assortment of slinky Fredrick's of Hollywood type women outfits, a leather whip, spiked heels, assorted plastic dildos and vibrators, condoms of all kinds, and about twenty different types of gels and creams. The armoire also held about twenty tapes.

"Throw me a tape, dawg, I'd like to see what kind of smut Dominique's selling to his customers," Bishop called as he headed toward the VCR.

I picked up the closest tape and tossed it to Bishop, who slipped it into the VCR and hit the Play button. The big-screen came alive with Dominique sitting in the leather chair smoking a huge cigar as he watched three sisters kissing, hugging, and playing with one another in his bed. One of the women whom I recognized as the lady hanging from the pole when I came there last, stopped admiring her partners' breasts long enough to ask Dominique to join the party. Dominique shook his head, and the girls continued without him.

Bishop was just leaning against the wall watching the scene as Micah took out one of her bugs and attached it to the underside of the bed, ignoring the on-screen antics.

"Dominique's doing better than I thought," Bishop said, speaking to no one in particular. "He's got to be making a small fortune on the side if he's doing what I think he is."

"What's he doing, Bishop?" I asked, knowing the answer but wanting it verified just in case I was thinking about the wrong thing.

"Smut videos, dawg. Lots of fresh meat, no real reason to give them a major cut of the profits, just a little liquor or coke, and it's on. The money has to be smoking."

"You think these are the same movies they sell outside the club on the weekends?" I asked.

"Why not? Clients drive up, enjoy the club then bring Momma a little taste of the club when he goes back home. The American way of doing business. I ain't mad at him," Bishop answered, actually sounding impressed with the way Dominique was working this. He also went back to the VCR, turned it off, ejected the taped and tossed it back to me. I replaced the tape exactly where I got it and closed the armoire door.

"Let's get out of here, folks. Our twenty minutes are almost up," Micah said, heading for the door with Bishop and me close behind.

Bishop closed the secret door and followed us down the hall and outside the building.

Before we got to the cars, Micah grabbed me by the arm and asked, "Would you like to go out to dinner tonight, handsome? Just you and me and no talk about any of this drama. I need the break."

The butterflies in my stomach started with the first words she asked, but my mouth said yes before I could interrupt it.

"Okay, love. I'll pick you up around eight," Micah added as she smiled at me genuinely and headed for her car.

I shook my head at my own stupidity and got into Bishop's car. I didn't know if he heard Micah's invitation for dinner, but he was quiet all the way home.

Chapter 31

Micah arrived at exactly eight o'clock. She called me at seven to remind me of the importance of a little laid-back time for the both of us and to make sure I had not changed my mind. I was on the phone with Gina at the time making sure that Ashley was doing okay, which she was. It's hard for me to admit, but I wanted some one-on-one time with Micah. I still had so many questions for her. I was intrigued by the unique life she'd led as well as the real reasons for her so-called attraction to me.

Micah blew the horn when she got to the house, and I jumped in her car, not knowing what kind of night we were going to have but feeling excited about the possibilities. Micah had asked me earlier to wear something casual because she had a surprise for me as far as dinner was concerned. So, I threw on a pair of black baggy Gap jeans, a matching black denim shirt, and some soft black leather slip-on shoes. Casual to me always means no belt and no socks, so I left those accessories at home.

I was pleasantly surprised to see Micah took her own advice and dressed just as comfortable as I did. Micah's blue jeans were ripped at the knees and a pretty beige cashmere sweater and mules completed her outfit.

"Good evening, handsome," Micah said softly as she reached over and kissed me lightly on the cheek.

"Why do you do that, Micah?"

"Do what, baby? Show you love?"

"I guess, if that's what you call it. It's the attention, the physical passes, and the emotional commitment you play with. Why me and why now?"

"Let's eat dinner first, love. I hate talking about anything as serious as your feelings for me and the ones I have for you on an empty stomach. So let's just enjoy the short ride and hopefully a great dinner, lover."

I wasn't going to start the night off by arguing with Micah, so I closed my eyes, laid back, and relaxed. Breaking and entering, planting bugs, and dealing with smut wasn't what I'd call a stress-free day, so the insides of my eyelids were a peaceful escape.

Before I knew what Micah was doing, we were parked in front of her door, and she had turned off the engine.

"Okay, love, dinner's waiting," Micah said nonchalantly as she opened her door and started up the stairs to her house.

I shook my head, got out of the car, and followed her. I should have known that when dealing with Micah, expect the unexpected.

As we entered her house I was immediately swept away by the intense earthy aromas that permeated the house. Micah's foyer and living room were illuminated by dozens of lit candles, in all shapes, sizes, and colors, scattered throughout. The warm glow took my breath away, and Micah's hand grabbing mine took me into her world.

"Come, love, dinner is getting cold."

Micah led me reluctantly into her dining room, which she had prepared in her own personal Micah chic. The table was set for two with paper plates, top-of-the-line paper plates, of course, jelly jars filled with melting ice complimented with purple spiral straws, and plastic cutlery. Micah looked at me and started to grin as she guided me to the table and sat me down. She trotted off to the kitchen and trotted back within minutes with four Chinese to-go cartons, a pitcher of red Kool-Aid and serving spoons on a big tray.

"Okay, love. In case you haven't figured it out I don't usually 'do' kitchen. But, I have the quickest fingers in the world when it comes to ordering fast food. Now here's what the young man with the fake accent delivered. We have General Chen's chicken, combination fried rice, hot-and-sour soup, and fat-ass egg rolls. Plus, a bunch of duck sauce to cover the taste of any cat meat they may be using," Micah said as she took her seat and immediately started dishing out the food.

I sat there completely amazed at the way Micah looked in candlelight, beautiful but vulnerable. I also sat there frustrated because I had allowed myself to be dragged deeper and deeper into her world. Before, I could continue to beat myself upside my own head, Micah grabbed my hand, closed her eyes, and started to pray.

"Lord, please bless this well-deserved meal and continue to guide me and my well-defined brother down the path that you deem appropriate for the both of us. Amen.

"Now let's eat, handsome, I have a special dessert waiting in the kitchen for you," Micah said softly as she began to eat her meal, ignoring my confused look.

There wasn't much for me to say at that moment, and my stomach was talking fiercely since I hadn't eaten anything that I could remember all day. So I gave in to the moment, grabbed the plastic fork and dove in. The food was delicious and hot so it didn't take long for me to forget the entire day or where I was or who I was having dinner with. Micah was a silent eater never saying more than "pass the egg rolls and duck sauce, please." It only took us about fifteen minutes before the cartons were empty, and my stomach had stopped growling.

"Thanks for dinner, Micah. As much as I hate to admit it, this was a well- needed meal for me."

"Anything for you, love, but the best is yet to come. I lied earlier when I said I don't 'do' kitchen. I do a little kitchen but only when it comes to dessert and breakfast. I hope you like chocolate because I made you a delicious chocolate cake. Would you like ice cream with yours or would you like to just spread your slice all over my body instead?" Micah asked, laughing at her own joke, as she slowly rose from the table and started to clean up our mess.

I reluctantly and lazily got up from my seat and pitched in, grabbing all of the junk Micah couldn't and following her into the kitchen. Micah's kitchen was built for a master chef, complete with stainless-steel appliances, a large island situated in the middle of the floor, huge stainless-steel pots and pans hanging from the ceiling, and a wraparound counter. Micah went straight to the garbage can and threw everything in, with me following her lead with my junk.

"Baby, please go sit down now. I can handle the rest of this, and I'll have dessert out in a second. Do you want ice cream with your cake?" Micah asked while pushing me toward a door at the opposite end of the kitchen.

I told her ice cream would be great as I halfheartedly left her in the kitchen after being pushed into the living room. This room was sparsely furnished for its size, having just a multicolored fabric sofa and love seat, an entertainment center that covered an entire wall, even though it only housed a combination thirty-two-inch TV/VCR unit, a stereo receiver, and a CD player. This room was also illuminated by dozens of candles.

I sprawled across the sofa, closing my eyes and hearing for the first time the sweet sounds of Sade flowing through the room. I didn't have long to wait before Micah came out of the kitchen, and before I could move or complain, she laid down besides me, spooning herself into my body. I wanted to say something or pull away but all I found myself doing was gently wrapping my arms around her waist and holding her tight. As we laid there, Micah ran her hand against my thighs and pushed herself even closer into me. My body loved the way this felt but my subconscious voice screamed out "traitor," over and over. We laid this way for what seemed like an eternity before I got the nerve to break the silence.

"Why do you do stuff like this, Micah?"

"There you go again, lover. What stuff am I doing this time?" Micah asked, sounding sleepy and a little hoarse.

"You try to give me so much of yourself, physically and maybe even emotionally. Being intimate without a real reason. Touching without a hint of it being anything more than just a touch but still more than a touch. Why me? Why now?" I asked, realizing that my voice was also low and hoarse.

Micah didn't say anything for a moment, but she did turn completely around, getting even closer to me, face-to-face. She looked deeply into my eyes as if she was searching for some great truth. At that moment she looked and felt so vulnerable.

"Noah, it's been months since your wife died, and I respect what you had with Andrea. I'm not trying to replace her, either. I can still hear you telling me about the way you and she flowed.

But, let's also keep this real. I like you, my brother. I love the things you seem to be. I love the daddy in you, I love your dedication to what you and Andrea had, I love the way you are willing to risk it all for the truth. But the reality is, Andrea's not coming back, and I'm here."

There it was again. Bishop, my pops, Gina, they all made it seem like I was living in the past but nobody handed me a manual on how long to grieve or when to allow another into my life. I felt like if I moved too soon I'd be tarnishing the love I shared with Andrea. If I stayed to myself, I'd be living in the past. And my body didn't make any of my decisions any easier. I was physically attracted to Micah. I would probably be attracted to her physically if Andrea was alive but Micah scared me, and I didn't know why. Lying here next to her, feeling her breasts against my chest, feeling her hand run across my face as she looked into my eyes made me want to run for the door.

"What are you thinking about now, Noah?" she asked innocently, if I could imagine her being innocent.

"You, and the way you make feel. Let me ask you a question. Can you give me a little breathing room? I know I can't bring Andrea back, and I realize more and more every day that my life has to go on. I also recognize the fact that you are a beautiful woman that has lived a life that I've read about in magazines. The bad thing is that I'm not quite ready for any woman, much less a woman of your caliber. You are a total package, more woman than I ever thought I could be involved with, especially after being blessed with Andrea."

"Noah, this is where we lose our connection. I am not asking you to marry me. I don't want to fill the spot that Andrea once held. Shit, in time I'll find a spot in your heart. Totally unique. Totally my own. What I want from you now is the warmth of your body. I'd love for you to ravish me and my soul tonight. I want you to make me complete in a physical sense, but I don't think you can handle that right now. I will give you your space, lover, but don't handcuff me. Let me flirt, let me dream about us, let me live a fantasy."

"And, if I go along with you and your need to embarrass me with your attentions, will you give me the room I need to grow into us becoming friends?"

"Anything for you, my love, but I have a favor to ask of you. Will you hold me, carry me to my bedroom, and rock me asleep in your big-ass arms?"

I thought about protesting and reiterating to Micah my stance on us just being friends, but the look in her eyes convinced me that it would be a waste of time to even go there. "Do I get to enjoy some of your supposedly excellent chocolate cake and some French-vanilla ice cream before we retreat to your bedroom?"

"As I've told you thousands of times in the past, baby, anything you want from me is yours." And, before I could stop her, Micah kissed me passionately on my lips, and my body went straight to mush. She then jumped up and headed for the kitchen as I sat there asking myself again for the hundredth time what the hell had I gotten myself into.

Chapter 32

It took two weeks before it all started to come together. Fourteen days, three hundred and thirty-six hours. It doesn't sound like a lot of time but to me and my bunch of misfits, it was an eternity. We drove one another crazy during this time, but I learned so much about the character of my friends. We rode Dominique around the clock. Between the three of us, we were able to watch most of Dominique's moves and goings-on. Micah was great at teaching us all how to be invisible. We worked with all three of the cars while always having at least two of us following Dominique separately.

Micah and I kept our distance, since the night we fell asleep on her sofa after eating cake and ice cream. I held her the entire night or did she hold me? All I know now is that she kept her word, never mentioning the night we spent together, snoring softly into each other's arms, to anyone. She also never stopped showing me love as she called it, but she was well aware of my feelings now, so she always stepped off right before she crossed our agreed-upon line in the sand.

Micah wanted to bug his car but the three-hundred-pound gorilla he employed as his personal driver and bodyguard never left the vehicle alone. Dominique always traveled with at least two other cars in his posse, a lead and trailing ride. His house was gated in a very secluded area of Cobb County. Security teams walked the perimeter with no set rhyme or reason. All of this combined made it impossible to get very close to the jerk.

But, the breakthrough we thought we were looking for came from Mia. She called Bishop on the cell about 4:00 A.M. after her fourth day working in the club. Bishop and I were waiting for Dominique to finish his Friday night fling with his two favorite strippers while arguing about the benefits and horrors of sleeping with as many different women as Dominique seemed to be involved with.

"Hello, handsome. Do you know how badly my feet are hurting me? You owe me a manicure and a pedicure every week for the next ten weeks, okay?" Mia commented to Bishop.

"As you wish, my love. How much money did we make tonight?" Bishop replied.

"We didn't make a damn thing, but I made about eight hundred dollars, and I got twenty business cards that I've already thrown away and the number of one of the young hot dancers here, so it's been a good night. But that's not why I called. How long have you sleuths been looking for Prophet and Darquita?"

"Awhile, why? You got something for us?" Bishop asked as I tried to overhear Mia's end of the conversation, which was relatively easy since her voice seemed uncharacteristically loud.

"I've been asked to dance in Prophet's new video tomorrow," Mia said.

"What? Are you sure? We've had no sign of him for months. Micah's going to shit a brick when she finds out. Did you hear anything about Micah's sister being there, too?" Bishop asked.

"Slow down, baby. And no I haven't heard anything about sista girl. All I know is that Dominique and his clowns are being very mysterious about the whole incident. They are suppose to page me an hour before they need me. Three other dancers and my beautiful self are then supposed to meet here, and we'll be taken to the site in a limo that they're providing. They are also giving us all of our outfits. I think the only reason they asked me was because I had the closest cup size to the girl who pulled out," Mia responded, sounding extremely proud of her unique breast size.

"Okay, baby. Why don't you go home and get some sleep? Call me in the morning, and we'll all coordinate this shit. I'm sure the whole gang will want to see Mr. Prophet and get to the bottom of this drama. The biggest problem we'll probably have is keeping Micah from unloading her nine in Prophet's ass before we get some real answers," Bishop said, laughing.

All I could say was "damn" when Bishop filled me in on all of the conversation I didn't hear, which wasn't much. Mia walked out of the door a few minutes later greeting the few men still hanging around the club. She walked to her car and pulled out without incident.

"Alright, boss, where do we go from here? I'm wondering if all that shit Micah's been filling us with is all fantasy anyway," Bishop continued.

"My wife being killed isn't fantasy. Micah getting attacked in her home and having to kill some fool isn't a lie! Micah being tortured and almost killed again isn't a dream. Having to watch a man killed is not a nightmare. Are you hearing me, Bishop?" I asked.

"Damn, dawg. I'm feeling you, so where do we go from here," Bishop responded pensively.

"Let's go. We'll all meet at my house at eleven in the morning unless Mia gets a page before then. This way we can set up whatever line of attack we need to get Prophet and Darquita away from Dominique. I'll call Micah myself and fill her in on the info Mia's dropped in our lap."

"Just don't be surprised if she blows up and just starts shooting folks if she sees her sister being held against her will," Bishop said as he pulled away with the lights off until we got about a block from the club.

"I'll handle Micah, Bishop. She knows there is more to this than just her sister. I need to know if this drama gets crazy tomorrow, will you have our back? You have as many secrets as Micah but I have to trust both of you without hesitation if we are going to bring this drama to a close," I said, looking at Bishop's profile lit up in the morning darkness by the other car lights that were on the road at this ungodly hour.

Bishop turned and gave me that crazy look of his and said, "Dawg, I'd take a bullet for you and the gang if it wouldn't kill me and there is no permanent damage but I don't think I'd trade my life for y'all asses though. We ain't that tight yet."

Chapter 33

It seemed like I dreamed of Andrea every night. But tonight there was a difference. Micah's in the dream with Andrea and me. Andrea and I were making love in my dream and Micah was standing at the head of the bed, watching and smiling. Andrea knew she was there, I could sense it, but she didn't care. She kept telling me how she always wanted me to be happy and loved, even if she was no longer a part of my life. As we continued making love, switching positions every time I was close to my peak or she was to her point of no return, she would repeat the same thing over and over. I wondered if I was just trying to convince myself that the desires I was feeling for Micah were okay. Did I subconsciously feel that I needed Andrea's permission to even consider a physical or loving relationship with another woman? I never dreamed of living a day without Andrea in my life, so I never dreamed about holding and loving another woman. My mind kept going back to the wedding vows we wrote to each other.

"I, Noah, take the love of my life, Andrea, as my wife and partner for all of eternity. I promise and commit to you my unselfish love, my desire to be all things to you, and to give you the space and support you need to continue to be your own woman. I promise to walk by your side as we enjoy the perfect days, to walk behind you and support you as you need me to support you in those things that you want to handle on your own even though the road may be rocky. I promise to also walk in front of you when needed to take those blows that only a man in love can endure for the love of his life. I pledge to you my unconditional love, my friendship, my trust, and my heart and soul, for I know in your hands these simple building blocks for our future will grow and prosper."

These words were written for two people who would grow old together. I never thought that I would spend one minute in another woman's arms after the moment I said "I do."

But the reality I face now didn't have an Andrea in it, and God knows I didn't want to face this world I exist in now. If it were not for my daughter, I wonder if I'd have the strength to continue. Was this the way all love ended, with one half dead and gone and the other half left to grieve alone? Did Andrea and I ask for this the moment we fell in love?

Chapter 34

We were all together by nine the next morning. Bishop had camped out downstairs, and when I finally awoke from my dream-filled sleep, Micah and Mia had joined him in the kitchen. They were all sitting at my kitchen table in various stages of preparing or eating breakfast.

"Good morning, handsome. Would you like me to make you a ham-and-cheese omelet?" Micah asked, looking absolutely ravishing in her black bodysuit.

"Sure, if you don't mind fixing one for me," I answered, taking a seat in the nearest available kitchen chair. I normally didn't wear anything to bed but since we started using the house as the command center for this little operation, I'd been sleeping in running shorts and a T-shirt.

"Damn, baby, you didn't offer to fix me breakfast. Why don't you like me? Is it my charming personality?" Bishop asked, smiling at the drama he was trying to initiate. He was dressed in some baggy stonewashed blue Gap jeans and a loose-fitting Morehouse T-shirt.

Before Micah could give him a smart-ass answer, the doorbell rang. "I'll get it, Noah, if you don't mind," Mia said, rising from her seat with a slice of bacon hanging from her mouth and heading for the front door as I nodded yes. She had on a pair of charcoal-gray baggy dancer's pants, black soft dancer's shoes and a plain white sweatshirt.

"So, Micah, did you get any sleep last night after we talked about Prophet and the video shoot?" I asked as she continued to prepare my breakfast.

"Handsome, I slept like a queen. This is the closest I've gotten to Prophet or my sister, so I ain't mad at the situation," Micah answered, blowing me a kiss and giving me one of her looks that made me feel uncomfortable for reasons I still didn't understand.

Before anyone could add anything else to the conversation Mia and Stephanie walked into the kitchen.

"Good morning, my fearless leader and friends," Stephanie exclaimed looking grim. She walked over to where I was sitting and gave me a hug.

Everyone said hello as I introduced Stephanie to the group. Many of them had spoken to her on the phone but only Bishop had met her personally when we first got together to fill her in on what info we had and what info we needed to get about Dominique and his club. "I've gotten all of the information the Internet and my contacts could get, and I think you'll be impressed," Stephanie said.

"Is there anything I can get you to drink before you get started, Stephanie? Or would you like some breakfast? I'm making Noah an omelet and can do the same for you if you'd like," Micah asked, mixing eggs as she spoke. She sounded so at home in my kitchen.

"Thanks for the offer, dear, but I've eaten already. I could stand some juice if you have any," Stephanie replied.

"Your wish is my command. Is apple juice okay? I think that's all we have left," Micah responded as she moved toward the cabinet and grabbed a small glass and started pouring the juice.

"That's great," Stephanie answered before directing her gaze to me. "Noah, this information was not easy to get but I enjoyed the challenge. My only problem is that you won't like most of it."

"Give it to me anyway," I replied, waiting for more drama.

"Dominique is very rich and very much in trouble. Over the last five years, he has been accused of almost every crime imaginable. Attempted murder, rape, money laundering, prostitution, embezzlement, bribing a federal judge, and assault to name a few, and he still has more than six charges hanging over his head as we speak," Stephanie said, addressing the whole group.

"Is there any crime he hasn't been charged with," Mia asked, looking confused.

"That's the problem," Stephanie continued. "He's been able to get off on all of the charges directed his way. He hasn't spent one day in jail as far as I can see, nor has he spent a day in court. Most of these charges were dropped for lack of evidence, or the witnesses changed their minds or just disappeared."

"A lot of those charges are of a federal content but most seem locally generated. Who was the charging officer in most of the cases?" Micah asked as she handed me a plate of grits and a ham-and-cheese omelet.

"That's a troubling spot also. All of the charges came from Detective Harris. I remembered his name from our first run-in with him at the airport and his stupid interviews after Andrea's death."

"I ain't surprised by that at all. Detective Dick's always had a hard-on for old Dominique," Bishop added.

"He's had that same hard-on for you also," I reminded Bishop, who in turn looked at me knowingly. "I want him in this if this goes ballistic," I continued.

"What the hell are you talking about? I don't want Detective Dick anywhere around us when we drop the nut on Dominique. Bad enough we got super cop working with us," Bishop said, looking at Micah. "Detective Dick is straight by the book. I ain't going into a lion's den having to worry about what's legal or illegal."

"Okay. You have a point, but Detective Dick can also give us legitimacy if we need it. I want to give him a little bait just so that if we need him, he'll be there," I continued, ignoring Bishop's fears but consciously acknowledging the legitimacy that Detective Harris brought to the table. I didn't know what was going to happen when we confronted Dominique and his crew but I did know it wouldn't be pretty or painless.

"I'm with you on that, dawg, 'cause that badge carries a little weight but if bullets are flying, that badge ain't shit," Bishop added.

"So is Bishop dropping a dime to him or will it be you, Noah," Micah asked as she took a seat next to me.

"Got to be me, baby," Bishop answered gleefully as he grabbed his cell phone and started dialing. "I love to yank Detective Dick's chain every chance I get."

"Hold on, Bishop. What are you going to tell him?" Micah asked.

Smiling viciously, Bishop said calmly, "Trust me, baby, and just listen to a true playa play his game."

Micah looked at me, and I shrugged my shoulders and waited to see how Bishop was going to play this card.

Bishop finished dialing the number, and we all waited anxiously. We didn't have to wait long because it seemed like Detective Harris answered on the first ring.

"Detective Dick, how ya hanging today?" Bishop said into the cell. Bishop listened for a few seconds before continuing. "I'm glad to see you're still breathing, old man, but I called for a reason. I got this huge ache to confess all of my earthly sins, and I'd like for you to be my savior and priest. Are you going to be available today?"

Bishop listened for another minute, his smile growing by the second. "Great, I knew you'd love to provide me a shoulder to cry on. You make enough money to buy a cell phone this year?"

Detective Harris said something, and Bishop laughed deeply then asked for the number. As Bishop cut off the phone, looking proud at his manipulation of Detective Harris, a sharp, shrill beep from Mia's side interrupted his moment.

Mia grabbed the beeper, checked out the number, and looked at us all solemnly. "It's work, so I guess I better get my ass in there." Mia rose and started for the door.

"Hold on, woman. You ain't going nowhere until I know we can get your cute little ass out of there safely," Bishop jumped in.

"Slow down, baby," Micah added.

"Alright, let's talk this through," Mia answered while taking her seat again.

"First things first," I started. "Let's finish listening to Stephanie. Is there anything else we need to know?"

"Yes, there's plenty more. The biggest surprise was the money this man's companies are bringing in and spending, especially his newest venture. He applied for another business license and started a music and talent company about six months ago. Dominique's name isn't on any of the original documents but it all ends with his signature and money in his bank accounts. In six months, Dominique's spent close to a quarter of a million dollars with not one dollar coming in that I can find."

"What's so unusual about that, Stephanie? Many businesses don't make a profit before the third year," I said, knowing that it took me at least that long to turn a small profit.

"You're right, Noah, as far as most businesses are concerned but we're talking about Dominique's businesses. He's all about making the dollar, and making it now. His past and current business history shows a man who only starts businesses that make money quickly," Stephanie continued, full of energy and info that she wanted to share. "He's just finished a one hundred and fifty thousand dollar recording studio in an old, abandoned warehouse near the closed Amtrak train station. I expect him to put that building into production soon. He doesn't show the character of a man who sits on his money if it ain't making a profit for him."

"I bet that's where the video is being shot," Micah added as Bishop nodded in agreement.

"And that may also explain why Prophet had come out of hiding. Dominique needed him to be recording immediately if he was going to start selling the guy's music and bring in the loot," Bishop said.

"Then that's how we'll play this," I jumped in. "We'll split up into three cars. Bishop, I want you to follow Mia to and from the club. If Mia can get the word to you on exactly where they're going without getting noticed then that's what she'll do. If the location is anywhere but the warehouse, it's up to you to get the new location to us."

"As you command, my fearless leader," Bishop replied sarcastically.

I ignored that last comment and continued. "Micah I want you to get the address of the warehouse from Stephanie and head over there. Check the place out and get as much info as you can. If we're going to interrupt their party, I want us to know what we're up against."

"No problem," Micah responded, looking off into space.

"Damn, dawg, I think sista girl's about to go off on the deep end. She got that killing look in her eyes," Bishop said, pointing at Micah.

Micah turned to look at Bishop and just smiled.

"Micah, I need you working with us, and that means if you see your sister, don't just walk in and grab her. We all have a lot at stake here, and you killing Dominique or anyone else before we can put this puzzle together makes all of our sacrifices moot," I said, trying my best to sound like I was in charge.

"Baby, if I had seen my sister before hooking up with you clowns, I would have shot everyone in the house, including Prophet and Dominique. Times have changed since then though, or maybe I've just changed, so believe me when I say that we'll go into this together, and we'll end it together. Is that good enough for you, lover?"

Before I could answer, Bishop smiled and said, "Sure, honey."

We all laughed, and Micah gave Bishop another one of her "I- can't-stand-you" looks.

"So what are you going to be doing while we're out here busting our asses?" Bishop asked, directing his question to me.

"I'm going to take my daughter to the park."

Chapter 35

I know this was selfish of me but I got into this because of family, and if I was going into the great unknown, I wanted to spend some time with my daughter and my dad.

When I got to my father's house, I walked in on Pops feeding Ashley her lunch. He looked so strange sitting at the table with this very little person cradled in his arms as he wrestled with a bowl of rice cereal mixed with a little jar of Gerber's bananas.

"You want to finish what I just started, boy?" my dad asked, sounding a little relieved.

"You know I do, old man," I answered as I took Ashley into my arms. Ashley knows my voice, and she smiled and giggled at me. My daughter has the most beautiful eyes, and they always seem to smile at me whenever I hold her in my arms or she hears my voice. Am I imagining this unique display of love from a child to her father, delusional in my fatherhood?

GJT Simpson

"Would you like some juice, Noah?"

"No, old man. I had a big breakfast with the crew this morning, so I'm feeling fine as far as my stomach is concerned," I answered.

"So, tell me what you and your crew got planned to end this thing so you can start being a full-time father to this pretty little girl again," my dad said, sounding a little disappointed.

"We're about to put this puppy to bed, Pops. We were able to get some great information on the location of Dominique, Prophet, and Darquita," I answered, trying to sound more confident then I was actually feeling. I then spent the next fifteen minutes explaining everything that had happened up until this morning and answering his questions.

"Damn, you and your friends have got farther along with this than I thought. I just want you to be careful, boy. Money makes people stupid," my father added after hearing the whole story.

"I will be careful, Daddy, but the reason I'm here is because I want to take Ashley to the park. I miss this little lady so much," I said as I got up, still holding Ashley, and started packing up her stroller.

"Awright, boy. I'll get her diaper bag. You make sure you fix her a cold bottle to take with you. It's kind of warm out there," Pops said, heading to Ashley's dresser drawer to get her stuff together and put into her Winnie the Pooh bag.

Ashley had dozed off in her stroller and was still sleeping peacefully by the time I rolled her out of the house. It was close to fall so the weather was cool even though the sun was shining warmly. Piedmont Park was only a couple of blocks away, so the walk was pretty nice. By the time I found a nice spot under a small group of trees, Ashley was stirring from her sleep. I spread out the blanket my dad had packed and grabbed her diaper bag.

As if on cue Ashley started to cry softly. I reached down to pick her up, and she reached up and swiped my nose. My daughter felt so great in my arms, and I couldn't help but smile. I relaxed on the blanket with Ashley sitting on my chest. She stopped crying long enough to grab my lips and pull at them gently, smiling and laughing as she mauled my poor kisser.

Being in the park with Ashley made it impossible for me not to think of Andrea and the life we had shared together. Before and during the pregnancy we would drive to Pops' house and walk to the park. We would always help each other stretch before starting our walk through the park. It took us a couple of trips to come up with the most challenging path to take but once we figured out where all the hills were, we were in business. Never wanting to take things easy, we would start off slow and see which one of us would be the first to increase the pace and push the other.

During this time we would talk about everything and anything. We planned our future on the path, we argued about politics and the direction of our people here, we planned our first child and all of the things "she" would accomplish. Andrea was always confident that the first child would be a girl. We always dreamed about the day we would have the chance to walk through the park with Ashley in her stroller and Andrea pregnant with our second child. As I enjoy this moment with my daughter I was again reminded of how much my life and my daughter's life had changed since Andrea's death. So many dreams and desires destroyed for reasons I still didn't understand. I still felt silly though. When I did get the answers I wanted, would I be complete? Would I stop the reminiscing? Would I be able to nurture and mold this little princess into the beautiful and complete woman her mother was? I was so scared.

I shook off the feeling and got Ashley's bottle and her little Gerber's green bean and applesauce jars out. Ashley wasn't very hungry so I spent the majority of the time begging her to eat just a little and dodging the excess baby food she either spit out or knocked off the spoon. Ashley laughed at me and grabbed at the spoon more than she ate off it. I finally got the point and succumbed to just letting her have her bottle of milk with a little bit of cereal mixed in it. I should have known better than to have tried to feed her again so soon after she had eaten at home, but I needed to do something. I had no problem getting her to devour the bottle. Andrea loved milk, and her daughter seemed to be following in her footsteps.

I guess I've put this day off long enough, so I packed my little brat up and started home. Pops was sitting on the porch and seemed relieved to have us back to the house.

Ashley was acting kind of cranky, and I figured she was a little sleepy so I stayed there long enough to rock her to sleep.

Pops gave me a final "be careful" and "finish this crap" look, and I was out of the door.

I felt a tingle as soon as I got close to my car. I realized too late that my internal warning buzzer was trying to tell me something. As animals whose ancestors lived on instincts for thousands of years, we are built with that "special gift" that can warn us of immediate danger if we're willing to listen. I heard the warning but I was a little too late when it came time to react to it. I felt the barrel in the middle of my back before I could see who was working it and someone else grabbed my arm. I started to turn around but a rough, raspy voice whispered in my ear, "Don't turn around, nigga. Just hand my boy the keys and walk over to the passenger side and let's slide into the backseat."

I hesitated a minute, and my new friend wasn't too happy about that so he shoved his gun a little harder into my back.

"Don't make me go into that house you just left and introduce myself to your old man, Okay?"

GJT Simpson

Chapter 36

No one said anything during the ride. I wasn't scared, but what I felt wasn't something I could describe. I believe I've fantasized like most black men about being this superhero who when put in a situation like this or if given a chance to run and save a family from a burning building like you see on TV, I would respond without fear or concern for myself. But I was concerned. I was worrying about my family as well as my friends, and myself but was just not scared. I didn't want to die, and for the first time since this nightmare began I realized that the people I was dealing with were more than capable of ending my life as they had Andrea's. What would my daughter do for a father then? No mother and no father, why didn't I think about that before? Maybe it did cross my mind, but I never felt like I wouldn't succeed in finding my wife's killer and bringing him to a justice that I could live with. I still believed that, and I now knew that the journey was almost complete and that the right person would pay for the loss of my wife. I must have been delusional.

As we drove through downtown Atlanta, I knew where we were going. It took us about fifteen minutes to get to the warehouse Stephanie had spoken about earlier. The warehouse looked just liked most of the other ones in this area except for the twenty-foot gate complete with razor-sharp barbed wire that surrounded the building and three armed guards waiting at the nondescript guardhouse. I had never seen guards like these before. Each one of these bruisers was at least three hundred pounds, had cornrow braids, and had three tattooed teardrops on their right cheeks. They were dressed in army-green fatigues, shiny black boots, with nines strapped to their thighs, pump-action shotguns slung over their backs and some form of machine guns that I didn't recognize in their hands. As we drove up to the gatehouse, two of the goons surrounded us on both sides while goon number three came to the window. The driver who hadn't spoken a word the whole trip rolled the window down and said, "What up, Malik? We got a guest for 'Nique."

"Nice car, Shaka. I think I want this one after 'Nique finishes with his ass," Malik answered. Malik's mouth was toothless but it shined in the sun. It looked like all of his original teeth had been removed and replaced with silver teeth, top and bottom.

"Damn, dawg, when you get the platinum grill installed?" Shaka asked, looking extremely impressed with Malik's abuse of his permanent teeth.

"Bonus loot came in handy this week, so I got it all fixed. My bitch loves this shit. She can't wait till I set her up with some of her own," Malik continued as he checked out his grill in the side mirror of my car. "I see you took Loco with you on this trip. You shoot anybody this trip, fool? "

Loco stared at him without flinching or answering his question.

"Yeah, the boss was feeling freaky this year as far as the Benjamins is concerned, but you need to leave Loco the fuck alone. Just 'cause that nigga ain't got no tears don't mean he ain't capable of killin' all you hard-leg fools," Shaka replied, looking disgusted.

"Nigga, who you fronting on? Yo' boy don't scare us. We got nine kills between us, and these tears is all you need to see to know we ain't fooling," Shaka continued, pointing to the tattooed tears on his cheek as his boys showed no sign that we were even there. Malik started to argue with him but just shook his head in disgust and pointed toward the gate saying, "Nigga, let us in. You know 'Nique don't like waiting on anybody."

Without waiting on a response Malik rolled up the window, and Shaka reluctantly gave the signal to one of his boys and the gate was opened. The other goon stepped away from the car as Malik pulled a cell phone from his pocket and started talking. We drove about one hundred yards until we were on the backside of the warehouse.

The warehouse was about four stories high with large windows that were painted over. There was a freight deck on one side, which was filled with three medium-size moving vans. There were four or five moving people unloading one of the vans while five armed guards watched their every move and two cameras posted above their heads watched them all. The moving people were unloading music equipment and props as well as a number of plain wooden crates.

Shaka stopped the car on the far end of the building where there was a set of stairs that lead to the second floor. My backseat guest still had his gun pointed at me and nudged me with the barrel to get out of the car once it stopped at the stairs. I followed his direction and stepped out. I was trying to pay attention to every detail as far as my captives were concerned. I was looking for a way out but I also wanted to get as many answers as I could find, and if that meant dealing with this drama then I would. I was confident that Micah was there somewhere and if she wasn't she'd be there soon. I was also sure that they were filming the video there, which meant Bishop and Mia would be close by also. I'm amazed at how I had learned to trust and depend on a group of people I had never even laid eyes on until a few months ago. I also believed in myself. If no one showed up to help me, I'd still get what I came for. I was going to get the man who killed my wife, and if I could, I was going to kill him myself. This thought had been working in the back of my mind since I started this; I just never wanted to say the words. Now that I was this close, I knew now what I had to do to be at peace: I had to kill the man who killed my dreams.

We started up the stairs in a single-file line with me sandwiched between my escorts. The door had a keypad lock. Shaka entered a code, and the door buzzed and opened. The floor was a wide-open space with a circular receptionist desk in the center of the room. No one was there now, and my escorts rushed me to a corner of the office with a very nondescript elevator. There was another keypad like the one at the door on the side of the elevator instead of the typical up and down buttons. Shaka entered a three-digit code that I couldn't make out, and the doors opened. The gun barrel nudged me again so I filed in with the rest of the goons. There were four floors showing on the panel and a single place for a key. Shaka took a key out of his pocket, inserted it in the lock, and turned it to the left. The doors closed automatically, and the elevator started and rose immediately. We ascended quickly, and within seconds the elevator stopped and the doors opened.

As I stepped outside of the elevator I entered a beautifully decorated apartment. The huge space was completely opened. Most of the furniture was ultramodern and consisted of an eight-foot black leather sofa with a matching loveseat on the far right-hand side of the room. A king-size platform bed covered with black satin sheets and about ten gigantic pillows occupied the left side of the spacious room. The floors were made from beautiful white hardwood reflecting the dim synthetic light that glowed from the lamps stationed from the open black wood rafters above. The room itself was unusually dark except for bright light that was concentrated on the center of the apartment. But it was Bishop tied to a leather chair in the center of the room with his face battered and his left eye swollen shut that got my attention and made my stomach turn. Mia was standing next to him crying softly. Before I could say anything, the elevator doors opened again and out stepped a smiling Dominique. "Welcome to my home, Mr. Houston, I'm glad you accepted my invitation."

Chapter 37

Without thinking I punched Dominique squarely in the nose. The punch was straight from the heart and guided through the muscles in my shoulders and driven by my legs. It was like I blacked out for a second. I had been holding this rage inside of me for weeks, and now that I was face-to-face with the man I blamed for the death of my wife and all of my dreams, I just lost it. Blood splattered everywhere. I tried to hit him again with a straight left-right combination, but Loco slugged me first, with the butt of his gun into the back of my head. I fell straight to the floor, and I was seeing stars everywhere, but it felt so good to hear Dominique moaning. I laid there waiting for the bullet that would send me to my wife but it never came. Through the haze I was experiencing from the blow, I barely heard Dominique's whisper, "Don't shoot his ass, Loco. Pick his silly ass up and sit him next to his boy."

I felt two sets of hands grabbing me roughly by the arms, and I just went limp.

"Damn, this nigga is heavy. Grab the chair so we can drop his ass," Shaka groaned as his voice strained from the effort of trying to move me.

I wanted to play out of it for as long as I could. As selfish as it may sound I just wanted to lull them into a false sense of control so that I could have at least one more shot at Dominique. They dropped me into the chair and started to tie me up but Dominique had other plans.

"Don't tie his ass up," Dominique instructed Loco as he took a seat on the bed, tilting his head to the ceiling and pressing a towel Shaka had given him to his nose, "Just keep a better eye on his ass. If he gets a chance to hit my ass again, I'll have all you niggas' dicks cut off."

Dominique didn't have to worry about that for the moment, there was too much distance between him and me for me to even think about grabbing him again. Shaka and Loco both had me by the shoulders, pressing me into the seat next to Bishop. Mia had moved a step back and was looking off into space as the tears continued to run down her face.

"Damn, 'Nique, why don't you just let me put a slug in both of these niggas' head, and we ain't got to worry about these silly fools anymore," Shaka said as he loaded a round into the nine he was sporting.

"Who running shit around here, Shaka? You or me?" Dominique asked, lowering his head and giving him a hard stare.

"You, boss. I just don't like the idea of these fools giving you grief, that's all," Shaka answered as he held on to my shoulder a little tighter, causing me to flinch.

"Glad to know I'm still the shit in this organization," Dominique added angrily as he stood and threw the towel on the bed and walked toward me. "Nigga, I don't like the look in your eyes, but allow me to let you in on a secret. You make another stupid move like that at me, and I'll have Loco shoot your little female friend here," Dominique said, pointing toward Mia. Mia had moved closer to Bishop and continued to stare off into space as she stroked Bishop's head, acting as if Dominique's threat held no reality to her and her existence.

Dominique leaned close to me almost face-to-face and just stared into my eyes. "That's better, nigga. I like the look in your eyes now. It's good to know you are so attached to your little posse here, but I got one question for you: Why the hell did you continue to stick your nose where it didn't belong?" Dominique asked, standing back up and turning his back to me.

"Does it really matter? Is there any answer I can give you that you would understand?" I asked bitterly.

"Loco, shoot his fucking ass and his friends. Then dump their asses in an incinerator. I done got tired of playing with their asses," Dominique spit angrily as he turned around and looked at me.

Before anyone could move, Bishop spoke for the first time. "Dawg, tell him why you doing all of this. Tell him why you ain't gonna stop until his ass is strapped and fried in the electric chair."

"Yeah, nigga, tell me. Tell me why my old friend Bishop here decided to run with you when he knew if I caught his sissy ass I was going to kill him."

I thought about the answer before I said anything, but it was still simple. "You killed my wife. You destroyed my future. You killed the mother of my child."

"Nigga, please. I ain't killed your bitch. One of my dawgs made a mistake and killed your lady. Big fucking deal. You middle-class motherfuckers got insurance, don't you? Why didn't you just collect the money and go on with your life instead of fucking with me and my organization? Nigga, do you know you fucking with potential millions. I could sell you another bitch that would marry your ass in a minute. I got a club full of gold-diggers looking for a middle-class nigga like you," Dominique raged on.

"My wife wasn't a bitch. She was my partner, and I loved her," I answered, feeling the hate for Dominique boiling within me.

"Oh, so you one of them niggas that take all that loving-my-mate-forever-or-till-death-do-you-part shit seriously?" Dominique asked, looking surprisingly happy at the thought of a man loving his wife the way I do.

"Yeah, 'Nique. My nigga got a serious hard-on for his wife. Don't you wish you were capable of loving a woman like that? Instead of treating them all like whores and disposable napkins?" Bishop asked, smiling through the pain that was clearly evident on his face.

"You got a lot of nerve, you two-bit pimp. Do this nigga know what you use to do before you got righteous on everybody?" Dominique asked, pointing at me but looking at Bishop as he asked the question.

"He knows what kind of nigga I used to be. But he don't give a damn. I believe the nigga would have worked with the devil himself if it would have gotten him close enough to wipe the floor with your ass," Bishop answered.

Before anyone could say anything Dominique moved quicker than I would have imagined and slapped Bishop roughly across the face, drawing blood from Bishop's lip.

Bishop looked up sheepishly while licking the blood with his tongue and said, "Damn, dawg, you still hit like a little bitch."

Dominique raised his hand to hit Bishop again but before he could strike, Mia screamed and wrapped her arms around Bishop's neck.

Dominique started to laugh, and looking at Bishop, he said, "Damn, you all some loyal motherfuckers to each other. Be glad to know you all going to die together," Dominique said, looking utterly disgusted at the bunch of us.

"Let me ask you a question, Dominique, before you finish playing God with our lives. What was so important that you had to have my wife killed?" I asked, feeling like the time we had left was growing short.

"Again, nigga, you got it all wrong. I didn't want to kill your wifey. I told that fool to kill that little pestering bitch that was looking for Darquita and causing me all that drama," Dominique started, and before he could say anything else the elevator rung and the doors opened. As if on cue, out of the elevator came a beautiful young lady who could have only been Darquita. She was the spitting image of her older sister except for the fact that she was only about five feet tall. She had on a pair of black spandex pants, a tight-fitting matching top and some four-inch pumps. Her face was without makeup, and it looked as if she had just finished crying. Hanging on to her arm was a tall, extremely slender, light-skinned young man. If one didn't look closely, he could probably pass himself off as a white guy. He had all of the typical white-man features, including the thin lips and pointed nose. The giveaway was the hair though. My brother had the nappiest hair I had ever seen on a black man. It was what my father would call cuckleberries. His hair was knotted and tight to his skull. I assumed this was Prophet because of the concerned look on Darquita's face when she would glance at him. Prophet had on a pair of round, thin eyeglasses, but he was still squinting. He had on some silver baggy pants and silver boots. His shirt was a black silk that fit his upper torso loosely. There was something extremely odd about his appearance but I couldn't put my finger on exactly what it was. Behind Prophet and Darquita were two more of Dominique's thugs.

"Perfect timing, folks. I was just about to explain to this little group here why you two are ultimately responsible for their deaths," Dominique explained, somewhat gleefully.

Chapter 38

As huge as the room was, it felt as if it had shrunk with the addition of Darquita, Prophet, and their goon squad. Darquita started crying as soon as Dominique mentioned the fact that he was going to kill us because of her and Prophet. Prophet showed no emotions at all, and it was then that I realized what was so different about him: Prophet was high. I had heard stories about rappers and other music geniuses that stayed drugged up most of the day but I had never seen it, and I honestly thought it was just a running joke.

"So tell us, ole great wizard. How come some drugged-out wanna-be rapper and his girlfriend is enough for you to kill us, Noah's wife, and God only knows who else?" Bishop asked defiantly.

"Money, nigga. Lots of money. Did you know this drugged-out wanna-be rapper's got over two hundred songs written and close to a hundred performed on a master that I own?

Do you have any idea how much Elvis, Tupac, and Biggie's people made after their asses were dead?" Dominique asked smartly.

Before anyone could say anything Dominique rattled on, pointing at Prophet. "This nigga here is platinum. I will have his ass on tour for about two years before he either retires abruptly or ends up a victim of a senseless crime of rage. Over that time I will be becoming more and more legitimate. Don't you know that the easiest way to clean dirty money is through a clean, legitimate business? Problem is the strip-club business is drying up. I got to buy off the local police, the newest mayor or councilman running an anti-nudity campaign, and the government always trying to take my liquor license. Music is damn near untrackable. I can run money in and out of this fool and no one would ever be the wiser. Then I can pad my pockets by charging crazy phat prices for anything I do for this fool because he don't want no money. A little weed, a little crack, a little coke, and he'll do whatever I ask."

"So your brilliant idea is to keep him high for two years till you make him a household name?" I asked incredulously.

"Yep. He only cares about weed and this little woman here," Dominique continued as he wrapped his arms around Darquita. She in turn pulled away instinctively. "Baby, you need to be good to me. I'm the only man that can keep your fine little ass alive. I done killed your sister, and I will kill you, too, if you start giving me problems."

For the first time since he stepped off the elevator Prophet showed us he was still alive inside of his doped-up shell. "No, 'Nique. You ain't gonna touch my baby. We got a deal, and making my baby happy is the one part you going to keep," Prophet said in a clear, deep voice that reminded me of the CD I had heard when this drama first started.

Dominique and his crew seemed surprised by Prophet's statement.

"Damn, this nigga still shocks my ass when I hear him speak. That voice is strictly platinum," Dominique stated, looking as surprised as he sounded. "Prophet, you know I'm just talking shit. I'll never hurt your pretty lady."

From the far corner of the room as if by magic, out stepped Micah dressed in black with a set of cocked nines in both hands. She was aiming directly at Dominique. "You got that right, motherfucker. You aren't going to hurt my sister or any of my friends again," she hissed.

Chapter 39

"Bitch, how the fuck did you get in here?" Dominique asked, looking at Micah and his so-called bodyguards expecting an answer.

"Dominique, please don't call me a bitch. My name is Micah, and that's my sister you've kidnapped," Micah answered, sounding extremely calm for the situation but never taking her eyes or her guns off Dominique. "And as far as how I got into your playboy pad here, you should have your lazy goons check all the crates before they unload them."

It all started to feel crazy and tense.

All of Dominique's goons had their guns directly on Micah, and she seemed to glow in the light. Darquita looked absolutely shocked to see her big sister alive and well. Before anyone could say anything, Dominique's chest rang. "Hold the fuck up, boys. Don't do anything until I tell you, or this stupid bitch start shooting first." Dominique spoke just as calmly as he reached for his inner coat pocket.

Micah seemed to take it up a notch as her body became more rigid but she didn't make a move as Dominique took out his cell phone.

"Can I answer this, pretty lady, without you shooting my ass?" Dominique asked Micah.

"Sure you can. Maybe after you answer that phone we can end this shit without me shooting you between the eyes," Micah answered just as calmly.

Dominique flipped the mobile phone and just listened. I could see all of the energy drain from his body before my eyes. He listened intently for a minute before dropping the phone.

"Loco, can you kill that bitch before she kills me," Dominique asked, never taking his eyes off Micah.

Before Loco could answer, Micah shot him right between the eyes. I didn't wait for the sound to clear the room. I grabbed Shaka by his gun hand and broke his wrist by pulling and quickly snapping it straight up in the air. Shaka screamed immediately and dropped to his knees. Two more explosions rang through the air, and I heard the bodies drop before I could see them. I knew Micah had shot the goons that had walked in with Darquita and Prophet. I kicked Shaka in the head, and he passed out immediately. I guess he should be happy that he was still alive.

Mia was on her knees untying Bishop, and Micah had crossed the room and had her nine right up against Dominique's temple.

Bishop was the first to speak as he started to rise from his seat, "Kill his ass, baby. If you don't, I will."

"Ain't neither one of us going to pull the trigger on this piece of scum. That honor belongs to Noah," Micah answered, handing me the other nine that wasn't pressed against Dominique's temple.

I took the nine into my hands, and it felt so good. Dominique looked at me and started smiling. "Nigga ain't got the guts for killin' like we do folks. If you didn't have the GBI and half of Atlanta's police force on their way up that elevator I would be a little worried for my life. But we all know this middle-class nigga ain't got the guts to shoot me in cold blood."

Before I knew what I was doing I had chambered a round into the nine and grabbed Dominique by the head and stuck the barrel directly into his right nostril. Dominique's eyes were as big as saucers, and I could feel him get weak in the knees. His nose started to bleed again. Before I could pull the trigger, the elevator door opened and out stepped my pops, Detective Harris, and every cop they could get into the elevator with their guns drawn.

Everything was quiet until my pops opened his mouth. "Boy, what the hell are you doing? Do you have any idea what you got waiting for you at home? Did you forget about that little girl that doesn't have a mother and can't afford to lose her daddy?"

My tears started as soon as he spoke the words. It was all over. This was what I needed to feel. I had done something to avenge the life that was stolen from me. I needed to go home. I looked at the fear in Dominique's eyes again, and I let him go. His body hit the ground with a thud, and I turned to my pops and said, "Let's go, Daddy. Give me a hand with Bishop though. He had a harder time with this physically than I did."

The cops immediately grabbed Dominique and roughly handcuffed his ass.

My pops smiled, and we both moved to stand Bishop up as Mia stepped aside to let us support our brother. Bishop looked up at me, and there was nothing I could say to repay this brother who believed in me and my need to make myself whole. "Just get me to my car, dawg. Mia will get me home."

I nodded in agreement, and we started for the elevator. Darquita and Micah were in a deep embrace. I'm not sure they even knew we existed. As we passed Detective Harris, he patted me on the shoulder and said, "I knew you two could do it. I'll see the both of you in my office tomorrow morning so that we can wrap this all up."

Bishop stopped and asked him, "How did you know we were here, Dick?"

Detective Harris looked sheepishly at my pops and pointed in his direction. "This gentleman called in to say his son was kidnapped at gunpoint, so we had all the justification to bust in here and put Mr. Dominique in jail for a long time."

My pops smiled, and we headed for the elevator.

Epilogue

Motherfuckers done fucked up all of my shit, but it ain't over. I've been fucked with enough for the day. They must think I'm some weak-ass businessman who's just going to go to jail and rot away for the rest of my life. First mistake these fools made tonight is to handcuff my ass from the front and put me in a car without one of their asses sitting in the back with me. Every cop in America knows you suppose to put a nigga's hands behind his back when you handcuff his ass. These unmarked, unscreened cars are great for the bigwigs to travel in, but they don't do nothing for a true killer. And believe me, before I ever got into the strip clubs, I was a true nightmare. But these GBI fuckers too busy worrying about their little middle-class lives at home to be afraid of a nigga like me. They patted my ass down good but not quite good enough. Most street cops would have looked for the key first, but like I said, these crackers ain't too bright.

First trick I learned in jail was to always have a handcuff key on a string around my neck. I sleep with it and I shower with it on. It was simple for me to just reach up while they talking about the Hawks and their free tickets and pop the key off of the string. I had the cuffs off in less time than it took me to punch the fuck out of the cop on the passenger side at the first stop we made and to strangle the driver before he could react. He looked so fucking surprised as I strangled the last breath from his body.

Now I'm going to do a little damage before I hop a plane out of this motherfucker. I'm going to kill that fucker tonight. He punched my ass in the nose, he ruined my business, and he damn near made me shit in my pants when he shoved that damn gun up my nose.

It takes me about twenty minutes to get to his fucking daddy's house. If I pull this off right, I'll get to let him watch me kill his old man and his daughter before I fuck his ass up, slow and easy. I pull in front of the door and all of the lights are off. Old-ass house so it shouldn't be any problem picking the lock and getting in. I can't wait to see his face as he realizes I'm about to fuck up his entire family. I get out of the car and check the guns I pulled off of the cops. I start for the front porch to check the lock, but the door isn't locked, and it opens quietly and easily. This shit is going to be so much fun. I start into the house but as soon as I heard that bitch's voice whispering good-bye, I know it was all over for me.

I spin around, hoping against hope that I can get my gun pointed in her direction before she can do anything to me, but the pain and lights that ring in my head are more than I could handle.

It takes me a second before I realize that I am lying on the floor in a pool of blood and vomit. I can't see it but I could smell it all. My whole right side is numb, and I can't tell if I still have the gun in my hand or not.

"Damn, another weak-ass wanna-be gangster that can't handle a little one-on-one batting practice with a sista," a soft and nasty sounding voice echo's in my head, that I know belongs to Micah.

I try to open my eyes and focus but it's hard. Micah seems to be reading my mind, because she grabs me by the hair, propping me up on the wall and slaps me across the face. Damn, this bitch can hit, which seems to help me focus through the pain. I try to wipe my eyes, but there's blood everywhere. When I do open them slightly I see her standing there with a Louisville slugger covered with blood in one hand and my gun in the other.

"You do know that you're going to die twice tonight, nigger," Micah spits in that low, raspy, fucked-up voice of hers.

I want to say something smart, be tough, go out like a true hard leg, but I can't get past the fact that I think I've pissed and shitted in my pants. This ain't how I imagined tonight. Why I got to go out like this? All my shit gone. The bitches, the money, the power. All because of this super bitch that walks through walls.

Micah steps back from my broken body and points the cop's gun at my face. I want to say stop, I want to beg her to let me be but she has other intentions.

"Before I put an end to your miserable life, let me tell you why you're going to die twice tonight. After I blow your face apart and your useless piece of a soul makes its way down to hell, I'm sure there's a beautiful woman with angel wings that you've never met waiting at the door to complete what I started. Tell her I've got Noah's back, and I hope she has a great time kicking your ass over and over before you cross to the other side."

I had no idea what this crazy bitch was talking about, but I didn't have long to figure it out, because she looked me straight in the face, and pulled the trigger.

the end

Prophet's World

Prejudice
Hatred
Crime
Poverty
The Four Horseman that we were born to battle

Ignorance
Greed
Lust
Selfishness
Laziness
The foot soldiers that were created to help keep us at one another
instead of at our given responsibilities that we earned through birth

The "man" has so many weapons at his disposal
Another generation with so many obstacles to face
Sex without consciousness or commitment or love
No respect for their life or the lives of others

Babies having babies who were children of babies
Three generations deep with no real idea of family
No reality or knowledge of a family core
No idea of the strength that a strong father can add to the mix
Never ever knowing a mother to hold and nourish them

GJT Simpson

What a shame!

The ones who have and can give are too selfish in their life of
Big Houses, Pretty Cars, Exotic Places

Too selfish to put our people's future in more competent hands
Too wrapped up in themselves to have a child
Too consumed by their personal pleasures to create a new generation
of Warriors that would and could make a difference
What a concept!

Prophet

Turn the page for an exciting preview of Gregory J.T. Simpson's next novel featuring Noah, Bishop and Micah in their newest adventure.

Urban Web Tales

A Creative Dreamers Creation
On sale Mid-2002

Chapter 1

"Good morning, Agent Dean! Thank you for granting me the pleasure of your presence!" Doc Young says sarcastically.

I really hate this short, fat, sick-looking woman, and I hate it even more when she calls me by my last name. I despise my last name, and she knows it, but when you're one interview away from being free, I mean totally free -- complete with bennies and my quiet money safely hidden, you can deal with almost anything, including being cool for the next thirty minutes and closing the door to this life of organized anarchy.

I take a seat in the huge black leather chair across from one of the biggest, solid wood desks I've ever seen. The desk had to be at least seven feet long, and it stood about four feet high by five feet deep. I love this humongous piece of furniture because it stands between the good Doc and me. It's very helpful in providing a physical wall separating us. The mental and emotional wall is always there to keep her out of my head, but the desk kept me from jumping across the room and simply wringing her fat neck when she started to piss me off with her silly-ass questions.

"Sorry about the missed appointments, Doc Young, I've been kind of busy," I answer with just a taste of sarcasm. I didn't want to piss off old girl, since I needed her to sign my discharge papers, but I didn't want to treat her any differently than usual, either. I've always felt she was as wacko as the people she was sent to treat.

"No apology needed, Agent Dean. I know that you just want to make this stage of your retirement a smooth transition. You look exceptionally well today so I guess it's okay to assume your new lifestyle is agreeing with you," Dr. Young continues not acknowledging my sarcasm.

"Since this is my last session, Doc, and I am looking so good today, why don't you call me by my first name? I'd even answer to Agent Micah if that makes you a little more comfortable," I say while looking her directly in the eyes for the first time today.

One of the major reasons I don't like looking at this woman is because I find her to be so damn ugly! Doc Young is only about five foot two but she is as wide as she is tall. Her expensive chair and desk can't hide the two hundred eighty pounds of lard she carries around on her tired bones. I know I shouldn't talk about fat people, but I'm not fat, and I can't understand why folks allow their temples to be so contaminated. I love my temple, and I am blessed with all of the reasons to respect my body and mind. My five-foot- nine-inch frame encased in my sculpted 36-24-36 inch body is a temple that, if I could package and sell, would make me a millionaire. By also being beautiful, fine, and well-trained in the art of survival creates a deadly combination when ninety percent of your superiors and peers are of the white, male persuasion. Being black also helps since most of these dummies still spend half of their existence dreaming about just how great it would be to get between my legs and into my heart. Or is it just between my legs?

Doc's also a terrible dresser and as usual she has on the same one-piece yellow-and-red flowered dress that had to be at least two sizes smaller than it should be. Her dress selection is nothing compared to the facial ticks and full body twitching that attacks her body continuously. My extremely curious Doc suffers from Tourette's syndrome. I saw a special on *60 Minutes* about this awful disease but had never met anyone suffering from it until I met my good fat doctor. She has all of the symptoms except for the vulgar verbal outbursts that I thought everyone consumed with this disease inherited. The people interviewed on the *60 Minutes* special would curse and scream repetitively, calling out the foulest names. They called blacks, niggas; women, bitches and whores, and cursed at anyone in hearing range for no reason at all. When I first realized Doc had Tourette's, I would sit there waiting for her to lose control verbally and scream out "nigga." I dreamed of shoving my fist down her throat at her first utterance but it never came to pass. I guess whatever drugs she was taking controlled that particular aspect of the disease better than it did the ticks and twitches, which was a blessing for her. As my previous reviews should have told her, I never liked being cursed at or called anything but Micah.

"Agent Dean, I am proud of your decision to break out on your own and join the average everyday world that you've worked so hard to protect for such a long time, but you must understand our hesitation in letting you pursue this endeavor."

"Did you actually use the word *letting*, Doc? I thought America was still the land of the free and home of the brave. And if I'm not mistaken, when I joined this *voluntary* organization, I was under the impression that leaving would always be an option," I say trying to sound disappointed in her and this organization.

"Of course you are allowed to resign, Agent Dean, but we do not want to release a loose cannon upon our unknowing public."

"Doc, is you saying that I be unstable?"

"Of course not, Agent Dean, but let's not fool ourselves. You have never been one to follow directions, and your decision to take an extended vacation a couple of years ago was very unprofessional on your part. You were in the middle of an assignment at that time, and we were lucky to complete the contract after you disappeared. And please lose the uneducated street vernacular, it really doesn't work for you," Doc Young continues, sounding confident in her control over my destiny but annoyed by my choice of words.

"OK, Doc, let's cut to the chase. You and I both know that the circumstances surrounding my unexpected vacation almost two years ago was a minor bleep on your little radar. I have done everything this organization has asked me to do, no questions asked. The least you and the silly folks in the suits could have done was grant me the time I needed, but you didn't, so I left. Done deal! I came back after I finished my personal business and I haven't missed a step. Now I want to leave this make-believe world we work in and maybe get married and have about ten kids," I answer, not believing the words that are coming from my mouth.

I've been a card-carrying player for my country since I graduated from high school. I was foolish enough to take that stupid little test that the government loves to give juniors and seniors, which was a little like the SAT or the ACT. I never intended to join any part of the armed services but my test scores went straight through the roof. The next thing I know, they're sending recruiters over in limousines to take me out to dinner and force-feed me the land-of-the-free-and-the-home-of-the-brave crap. And let's not forget their favorite hook, about how much my government needed people like me to help keep our world free. I was so naïve back then. Now I'm hard and cold, and I like it.

"Agent Dean, would you like to respond to my last comment?" Doc Young asks, sounding a little annoyed.

"Sorry, Doc, I was just drifting a little. You know what they say about us geniuses, we have such a short attention span. Could you repeat the question?" I ask, trying to sound as professional as possible but I can see Doc's face turning redder and redder, which is really hard for a woman as pale as she is.

"Agent Dean, I understand that you think you're God's gift to this agency but I am here for one reason, and one reason only. And that's to keep you and your geniuses sane. I listen to you and your peers' horror stories. I hold your heart in my hands as you cry and talk about the breakup of your families or the loss of your partners. Then I slowly and carefully put you warriors' back together again. That's my job, but listening to you and your depreciating comments is not in my job description. I will sign your release papers, but I want you to do one thing for me."

Before I could ask her what she wants, Doc asks me the one question every agent I know hates to think about much less discuss. "How many civilians have you exterminated that were not part of the package?"

I thought about a couple of smart-ass answers I could have given but the guilt that even I have a hard time keeping locked up gushed to the surface. I am an expert on Micah, so this little show of emotions is against everything I have trained myself to be. I knew the game when I started, and I played it in an emotionless vacuum, a vacuum that has allowed me to keep my sanity no matter what mistakes I made today or yesterday.

"Yes, I've made some mistakes, and some civilians paid the price for being in the wrong place at the wrong time. Yes, it does hurt, and it keeps me up some nights, but that's life. But you know all of this, so I'm figuring you're trying to induce a little mental pain before you send me on my way, right? But it's all good," I reply, gaining more of my composure with the sound of every word that comes from my mouth. I don't like for anyone to pull my strings no matter what the hell is going on.

"So the death of Diane hasn't been any more demanding on your psyche than the usual bouts of bad dreams?" Doc asks, sounding as if she really cares.

"So, is that the name you've given her, Doc? Because, if I remember correctly, we never did find out who she was or her given name," I say drifting back off to that fucked-up day.

The Doc sits there silently waiting for me to continue the conversation and I guess ignoring my question along the way.

"Before I answer your question, Doc, answer me this since it seems like you're going to ignore my last inquiry. Is this your last dagger? The one that releases me of all of my earthly responsibilities to you and the group?" I ask, making eye contact for what I hope will be the last time.

"As you wish, Agent Dean. Just tell me how the death of an innocent eighteen-month-old child affected you, and I will set you free."

"OK, boss. You want to hear my gruesome tale for the hundredth time? Here we go: Little Diane was eighteen months old on the day I accidentally killed her. As you know I was in pursuit of some right-wing racists who had buried themselves in their cabin in a remote and isolated section of Montana. Our Intel gave us bogus information and that's where the problems first started. We were told the house was full of angry white boys who couldn't get it up or keep it up, so we were given the red light to shoot first and ask questions later. When you've robbed twelve banks in eight states and killed ten bystanders in cold blood just to make a point, our government tends to get a little medieval on your ass. But from the security of your big desk, I'm sure you know all of that already, don't you, Doc?" I ask, stopping my story and getting in a last dig myself. Desk jocks have always been made to feel like second-class citizens, and I wanted my dear Doc to understand that the field is where the real work is done.

Before the Doc could say something in her defense, I continued my story.

"We had smoked most of them out and were packing their asses away when I noticed some movement from a corner of the house. I instinctively started in that direction without calling for assistance, and that was the second mistake. I rounded the corner and some big-ass white boy about six foot nine and weighing close to three hundred and twenty five pounds of muscle was trying to sneak into the forest. I pointed my company issued nine at him and told him to stop. The fool turned around and looked me dead in the eyes, and that's when I saw the small black box with a flip switch in his left hand and the baby snuggled in his right. He just smiled and started rambling about women and niggers taking over the world. The baby started crying, and he moved her closer to his chest. Dumbass continued rambling on about how he had enough explosives buried around the cabin to kill all of us, and all he had to do was hit the switch."

"Now, Doc, you've been working with me long enough to know that I have no patience for assholes, so when he raised the box to show me what kind of power he had, I shot his hand off. Damn, he looked surprised when his hand was hanging from the little piece of meat left on his wrist, and the box had fallen harmlessly to the ground. I was feeling a little smug as I approached him, and that was the third mistake. I didn't see the other piece in his waistband, so when he just dropped the baby and fell to his knees, all of my attention went to the baby, the last mistake of the day. He grabbed the pistol and fired at me. Clean shot at point-blank range. Center mass. I was stunned and fell backwards but I locked in on his ass and emptied my clip. Center mass, but my friend wasn't blessed or prepared like I was because he wasn't wearing a Kevlar vest. He hit the ground with a thud, and the impact of his big ass dropping caused his gun to fire off one last shot. The baby wasn't wearing Kevlar either, and his bullet ripped her apart."

I stopped talking long enough to see Diane's body splashed all over the forest as I had seen it so many nights since that time. I never learned her name or who her parents were but she became my lost child.

"They cleared me of all responsibility but we all know I was working outside of the company rules. Her death was on me. Story told. Can I go now, Doc?"

"Of course you can, Micah, and I truly wish you and the people close to you all of the luck in the world."

LOVE AND PROPS!!!

This is a section that is long due. I owe a number of people for their support and positive influence, which has allowed me to make my dream of being a published author a reality. There is no order of importance in this list because every person mentioned here played a part in providing me a foundation for making my dreams a reality.

Cree, Logan, and Chase, you kids make being a daddy the greatest event in the world.

Janet, the final piece to the puzzle that has made me complete.

I started this book almost two years ago in a cabin with the support of a very good friend. Sonia, you've taught me so much, and for this I will never be able to totally pay you back.

Dione, twenty-five years and counting, you know the score.

My daddy, who sat next to me and told me the story that has always made me want to chase my dreams until I caught them and made them a reality.

Gloria, you helped me put this drama together and without your ideas and criticisms it wouldn't have been completed.

Special thanks to all of the book clubs that took their time to read, review and comment on my first work of art. Your added voices helped me to create a book that WE can be proud of.

Final thanks to, Chandra Sparks Taylor, the best editor on God's green earth.